"You Were Always Good At Running, Ava."

She slowly turned and faced Jared. "I didn't think you'd care if I left—or notice for that matter."

His eyes darkened. "I noticed. Your husband here?"

Her pulse skittered as she was reminded of the lie she'd been forced to tell.

"We're not together anymore," she said quietly.

"You walk out on him, too?"

Ava took a deep breath. "I understand that you're angry with me, but that's no reason to be downright cruel."

"I'm not angry at you, Ava. You have to really care about someone to be angry with them."

She felt her throat tighten as tears threatened. "Look, you obviously don't want to see me. So let's just try to steer clear of each other."

Ava hesitated, then turned to leave. But he was right behind her, his large hand covering hers on the knob.

"Let go of the door, Ava," he said. "This time *I'm* going to be the one walking out first."

Dear Reader,

We're so glad you've chosen Silhouette Desire because we have a *lot* of wonderful—and sexy!—stories for you. The month starts to heat up with *The Boss Man's Fortune* by Kathryn Jensen. This fabulous boss/secretary novel is part of our ongoing continuity, DYNASTIES: THE DANFORTHS, and also reintroduces characters from another well-known family: The Fortunes. Things continue to simmer with Peggy Moreland's *The Last Good Man in Texas,* a fabulous continuation of her series THE TANNERS OF TEXAS.

More steamy stuff is heading your way with *Shut Up And Kiss Me* by Sara Orwig, as she starts off a new series, STALLION PASS: TEXAS KNIGHTS. (Watch for the series to continue next month in Silhouette Intimate Moments.) The always-compelling Laura Wright is back with a hot-blooded Native American hero in *Redwolf's Woman. Storm of Seduction* by Cindy Gerard will surely fire up your hormones with an alpha male hero out of your wildest fantasies. And Margaret Allison makes her Silhouette Desire debut with *At Any Price,* a book about sweet revenge that is almost too hot to handle!

And, as summer approaches, we'll have more scorching love stories for you—guaranteed to satisfy your every Silhouette Desire!

Happy reading,

Melissa Jeglinski

Melissa Jeglinski
Senior Editor, Silhouette Desire

Please address questions and book requests to:
Silhouette Reader Service
U.S.: 3010 Walden Ave., P.O. Box 1325, Buffalo, NY 14269
Canadian: P.O. Box 609, Fort Erie, Ont. L2A 5X3

REDWOLF'S WOMAN

LAURA WRIGHT

Silhouette®
Desire

Published by Silhouette Books
America's Publisher of Contemporary Romance

SILHOUETTE BOOKS

ISBN 0-373-76582-7

REDWOLF'S WOMAN

This edition published by arrangement with Harlequin Books S.A.

® and TM are trademarks of Harlequin Books S.A., used under license.
Trademarks indicated with ® are registered in the United States Patent
and Trademark Office, the Canadian Trade Marks Office and in other
countries.

Visit Silhouette Books at www.eHarlequin.com

Printed in U.S.A.

LAURA WRIGHT

has spent most of her life immersed in the worlds of acting, singing and competitive ballroom dancing. But when she started writing romance, she knew she'd found the true desire of her heart! Although born and raised in Minneapolis, Laura has also lived in New York City, Milwaukee and Columbus, Ohio. Currently, she is happy to have set down her bags and make Los Angeles her home. And a blissful home it is—one that she shares with her theatrical production manager husband, Daniel, and three spoiled dogs. During those few hours of downtime from her beloved writing, Laura enjoys going to art galleries and movies, cooking for her hubby, walking in the woods, lazing around lakes, puttering in the kitchen and frolicking with her animals. Laura would love to hear from you. You can write to her at P.O. Box 5811, Sherman Oaks, CA 91413 or e-mail her at laurawright@laurawright.com.

One

"**H**e's back."

At her sister Rita's words, Ava Thompson felt her heart drop into her pink satin pumps. "Who's back?"

"The ever-gorgeous Jared Redwolf, that's who," Rita supplied with a smile.

From atop her white-carpeted pedestal at Benton's Bridal and Formalwear, Ava stumbled sideways, letting fly a barely audible, "Ouch," as Mrs. Benton accidentally stuck her with a pin.

"Hold still now," said the older woman.

Barely hearing the good-natured reprimand, Ava stared down at her sister, her large green eyes severe. "What do you mean, he's back? Back where?"

"Here in Paradise," Rita said calmly, standing in front of the three-way mirror, fluffing her long, tawny curls. "He's across the street actually. When I went for coffee I saw him go into the diner." With a mischievous grin, she added, "And who could blame him? Did you know they have a patty melt, fries and a cherry cola, all for just $2.95 today?"

"Those patty melts are pure horse meat," Mrs. Benton stated flatly as she pinned the hem of Ava's stunning off-the-shoulder A-line number that her younger sister had designed to hit just above the ankle.

"Horsemeat." Rita laughed, her dark-blue eyes sparkling. "That's not true."

Mrs. Benton shook her head dejectedly. "And to think, we're living in beef country."

They weren't fooling anyone with their calm discussions of patty melts and cherry colas, Ava thought, taking in the pair's secret glances. From the moment Rita had mentioned Jared Redwolf, Ava had felt the two women's eyes on her, watching her like conspiring hawks—wanting to see her reaction to the news and wondering if her life was flashing before her eyes because of it.

A life that everyone in Paradise had known about. A life Ava had left four years ago.

A life she'd thought about every day since then in her small apartment on Manhattan's Upper West Side.

The dated air conditioner against the ratty lavender wall sputtered and coughed as the Texas heat slowly invaded the room. Ava eyeballed her sister in the mirror. "I thought you said he was going to be in Dallas for the entire two weeks, Rita. 'I have it on good authority,' you said. 'I swear, you'll never run into him,' you said."

Rita shrugged. "Hey, what can I say, big sister? That's what he told Pat Murphy at the post office." She grinned, then placed a bridal veil over her face.

"Maybe he heard you were back in town for my wedding and changed his mind."

Mrs. Benton inhaled sharply, then looked up at Ava with eager, expectant eyes.

"Not a chance." Ava glanced from one woman to the other. "The man despises me."

"Despise is such a strong word," Rita said.

"I think we should stop talking about her old beau for a moment," Mrs. Benton said to Rita. "She's moving about and I need to get a clean hem here. I sure don't want to be the one catching heck if your maid of honor walks down the aisle in a crooked dress."

Rita smiled at the woman. "How about I blame it on a certain six-foot-three Cheyenne god with a killer smile?"

Ava rolled her eyes. "He's *half* Cheyenne."

"And what a half," Mrs Benton said on a sigh, then quickly returned to her hem.

Nothing had changed, Ava mused. The women of Paradise still drooled over Jared Redwolf. But were they still too afraid to show it? she wondered. Now that he was a millionaire and a financial genius with famous clients flying into to see him every week, were the ladies in town willing to overlook his heritage?

The scent of an old wedding bouquet hanging from the ceiling permeated the increasingly humid air. Johnny Mathis crooned a plaintive love song on a small radio in the corner. And Ava felt as though she were suffocating inside her pretty satin bridesmaid dress.

Jared was at the diner. So close by she could almost feel him, breathe in that heady scent of sun and sweat he always possessed. She wanted to see him, God help her. But she knew how dangerous that would be. He would have questions and he would demand answers. Lord, what if he'd already heard she was back in town?

Beads of sweat trailed a path down her neck. She needed to get out of the shop. She couldn't risk running into him, not yet anyway. Not until she was ready to tell him about...

She swallowed the thought, looked down at Mrs. Benton. "I'm really sorry, Mrs. B., but I'll have to come back later."

The older woman frowned. "What? Why?"

"I have to go back to Rita's."

"For what?" Rita asked quickly.

"I need to check on—"

The bell located above the door of the shop's front entrance chimed merrily, interrupting Ava's bogus explanation. She glanced up into the three-sided mirror to see who had come in. Through the generous slit in the curtain behind her, she glimpsed a man walking through the shop door like he owned the place, as though the modest storefront was too small to contain him.

Ava froze, but against her ribs her heart pounded violently. Just ten seconds more and she would've escaped him.

Jared Redwolf.

Without thinking, she reached up and released her long, blond hair from the rubber band that had held it tightly in place all morning.

Jared was here. Though to her, he'd never left—her memory or her thoughts—for the four years she'd been away from Paradise.

Time seemed to slow. She put a hand to her mouth and exhaled, swearing that she could still feel the pressure of his lips on hers as he raked his callused palms up the bare skin of her back.

She tried to swallow, tried to breathe correctly. But it took significant effort. After all, she hadn't seen him face-to-face in such a long time, and this was not how she'd imagined their reunion.

"I'll be out to help you in a minute," Mrs. Benton called, without looking up as she fitted another pin, no doubt hoping to finish Ava's dress before she could run away.

But Ava was going nowhere at the moment. She was bolted to the pedestal, watching Jared as he stopped at a display of bolo ties, handling one in particular with great reverence. She felt free to look at him because she knew he hadn't noticed her through the slit in the curtain.

Free, but certainly not easy.

Her back to him, she just stared into the mirror, her gaze moving over him like an animal who hadn't seen food in days. Like the first day she'd seen him driving cattle on her father's ranch—bulging muscle and covered in sweat as he sat atop the fierce palomino he'd broken himself.

He'd taken her breath away.

If it was possible, he looked even more handsome today than she remembered. Dressed more like a cowboy than a multimillion dollar businessman in a blue chambray shirt, faded jeans and boots, he was easily the best looking man in Texas. Who was she kidding? He was the best looking man in the world. He was far past six feet now, with a man's body. Long and lean and hard. He'd let his thick, black hair grow past his shoulders, his high cheekbones were more prominent and his eyes, those heavy-lidded steel-gray eyes that charmed, thrilled and terrified you all at the same time, were cool and calm.

But of course, he hadn't seen her yet.

"Just here to return the tux, Mrs. Benton," he called out.

Rita gasped at the voice that was far lower, but just as seductive as Ava had remembered. So did Mrs. Benton, but she quickly recovered before calling out, "You can bring it back here, Jared. We're all decent."

"No." Ava fairly cried at the woman, panic welling up inside her.

Rita reached up and touched her hand, gave it a reassuring squeeze. But the gesture helped little. Ava felt as if her chest would burst. She couldn't see him now, or ever again.

Her gaze darted right and left as she searched for somewhere to hide, but there wasn't time. He was coming.

Every muscle in her body tensed.

Not now. Not like this.

But the white curtain parted anyway and Jared Redwolf walked into the circular space, a dark garment bag slung over one broad shoulder. Ava felt her breath catch at the sight of him, so dark and masculine, bracketed on both sides by pure femininity: racks of snowy-white wedding dresses. What would he think when he saw her? she wondered, apprehension threatening to choke her as she turned to face him. What would he say?

The only sign that Jared Redwolf wasn't a full-blooded Cheyenne was his full lips, but when his gaze landed on Ava those lips thinned dangerously.

Mrs. Benton cleared her throat. "I'll take that suit and get your receipt, Jared. Be right back, girls."

Ava barely noticed her departure. She couldn't tear her gaze from the man who'd ruled her mind since puberty. She simply stared at him as the only sound in the room came from a wily DJ announcing the time and weather on the radio.

Ten a.m. and hot as hell.

Ava felt another bead of sweat fall from her hairline to her neck, then snake down her back.

It was the weather, not her relentless attraction for Jared Redwolf that caused this reaction, she told herself as she watched his eyes blaze fire and his jaw twitch as he stared at her.

Finally she gathered her courage and found her voice. "Hello, Jared."

But he said nothing, just continued to stare at her as though she were an apparition—and a very unwelcome one. She felt like a caged animal in her pretty pink satin gown that hadn't been fitted to flattering yet.

Awkwardly Rita cleared her throat. "So, Jared. Back from Dallas early?"

"Too early, it seems," he said, his tone bordering on venomous.

A tight knot formed in Ava's stomach. But she understood his anger, and tried once again for polite conversation. "Jared, listen, I—"

"By the way, Rita," he interrupted, ignoring Ava. "Congratulations on your wedding."

Rita smiled halfheartedly, her gaze flickering toward her sister. "Thanks."

"I'd like to get you and your fiancé something, but—"

"We would've invited you, Jared, I just didn't think you'd be in town," Rita explained awkwardly. "But now that you're back, you're more than welcome to come.''

Ava felt her mouth drop open. This wasn't happening. She'd been so careful with her plans in coming here.

"I appreciate the thought," he said. "But I don't think so." His gaze was intense—and back on Ava.

"Sakir and I would love it," Rita insisted.

He shook his head. "Thanks, but I can't do it. I have a desk full of work and a client flying in that night."

"It'll be just a few hours."

Ava clamped a hand down on her sister's shoulder. "If he doesn't want to come, he doesn't want to come. Don't force the issue."

The humidity was barely noticeable when compared to the weight of sentiment that passed between her and Jared. His eyes had turned from fuming black to watchful cool steel and Ava felt that familiar stirring deep in her belly. The one she'd hoped she'd feel again, but prayed she wouldn't.

He could rile her from a hundred paces with that look, always would.

"What time did you say the ceremony was?" he asked Rita, though his gaze remained on Ava.

"Two o'clock," Rita offered.

He nodded. "Maybe I will stop by."

Clasping her hands together, Rita looked from one to the other. "Well, you could drop by the house and pick up an invitation if you want."

Ava's throat went bone dry. What was her sister playing at? Jared couldn't come by the house. Her gaze flickered to his. "You can just send it to him, little sister. I'm sure it won't get lost in the mail." She took a breath and added, "If you send it out today it will get there—"

"I'll come by and get it," Jared stated firmly.

The clang of Mrs. Benton's ancient cash register sounded. "Give me just one more minute, girls," she called from the other room.

Ava didn't have any more minutes left. "I have to go," she said firmly. A few years ago, she would've just remained until the very bitter end of this torture. A few years ago she'd been an idiot. But not today. She'd been through way too much in the past four years to allow these three people to tear apart her small sense of confidence. "I'll see you back at the house, Rita." Without looking at Jared, she stepped down from the pedestal, grabbed her purse and headed out of the curtained room just as Mrs. Benton was heading in.

"But the dress…" Mrs. Benton called after her, but Ava didn't listen, she needed air, she needed—

So intent was she on escape, she actually gasped when she heard the deep baritone from behind her say, "Running away again?"

Halfway to the front door, halfway to safety, she froze. That voice now filled with cold sarcasm had once told her how beautiful she was.

"You always were good at running, Ava."

She slowly turned around and faced him. "You didn't say one word to me in there. I didn't think you'd care if I left—or notice for that matter."

His eyes darkened and a muscle in his jaw twitched violently. "I noticed."

She wasn't exactly sure if they were talking about the dressing room or the past four years. "What can I do for you, Jared?"

"Not a damn thing."

"Then I'll be going."

"Your husband here for the wedding?"

Her pulse skittered in her blood as she was reminded of the lie she'd been forced to tell before leaving Paradise. "We're not together anymore," she said quietly.

"You walk out on him, too?"

Ava took a deep breath. Jared had a right to be angry with her, but she wasn't going to accept barb after barb. Living in New York, having a child and a high paying interior design job had really changed her. No longer was she a pushover to her father, to Jared—to anyone.

She took a step toward him. "I understand that you're angry with me, but that's no reason to be downright cruel."

"I'm not angry at you, Ava." His dark eyes bore into her. "You have to really care about someone to be angry with them."

She felt her throat tighten as tears threatened. She realized with a start that she'd actually formed a fantasy over the years about seeing him again. And this was so drastically far from that fantasy it was almost comical. She and Jared would never be together again. He despised her, and she imagined that even a full explanation and an apology wouldn't make much of a difference. The man had turned cold and hard.

But it wasn't just *her* feelings, *her* heart anymore. She had more to protect now. She straightened her shoulders. "Look, you obviously don't want to see me or talk to me. Let's just pretend this never happened, pretend we never had this encounter and try to steer clear of each other. I'll only be here a couple weeks. So that shouldn't be too hard."

"Are you telling me not to go to your sister's wedding?"

She swallowed hard. "Not telling. Just asking."

He nodded stiffly. "Then I won't be there."

Ava hesitated for a moment, then turned to leave. But he was right behind her, his large hand covering hers on the knob. Her breath caught at the feel of him, at his closeness. The scent of leather and heat and pure maleness emanated from him, heightening her awareness. For a moment, it was as if time had never passed. He felt familiar and wonderful, his scent intoxicating. She glanced down at his tanned fingers practically interlaced with her own.

"Ava?" he said, removing his hand from hers.

She looked up at him. "Yes?" He was so close she could feel the solid wall of his chest grazing her shoulder. She could feel his heat, his overwhelming strength. A combination that had branded her many times before.

His gaze traveled from her neck to her mouth, then up to her eyes. "Let go of the door." He raised a brow. "This time I'm going to be the one walking out first."

Jared drove his truck down the dirt road like a madman. Well, that's what he was, wasn't he? He'd just come face-to-face with the one woman he couldn't forget—the woman who'd betrayed him.

The wild beauty, he'd called her back then. And at twenty-six, she hadn't changed much—only filled out in all the right places. High breasts and curved hips with that slender white neck that had always driven him nuts. Those tiny freckles that were sprinkled about the bridge of her nose were still visible, but had faded somewhat. Her honey-blond hair was longer and more

lustrous than he remembered, but it still held the fresh
scent of daybreak.

Damned if it hadn't taken everything in him not to
run his hands through it when he'd stood beside her at
the bridal shop door.

He knew that she'd be here for her sister's wedding,
but the idea of Ava Thompson returning to Paradise
was just something he hadn't wanted to think about—
couldn't ever think about—if he expected to survive
his days and nights.

The first year she'd been gone had been hell, he
recalled, as the dull ache in his chest turned razor-sharp
like the spines of the cactus that lined the road outside
the truck's window. He could still remember that morning like it was yesterday. That morning when Ben
Thompson had met him out in the south pasture and
told him that he knew about Jared and Ava. Ben had
told him that his daughter had left for New York to
marry another man, someone her equal, and wasn't
coming back. Jared had been just twenty-four then. A
poor ranch hand who was working his way up in the
numbers business and wanted nothing more than Ava,
a few hundred acres of his own and a future in finance.
But no matter how much he'd wanted to go and find
her, fight for her, he hadn't.

She'd wanted another man.

She hadn't wanted Jared.

And neither had her father, Jared had quickly
learned. Ben had booted Jared and his grandmother off
of the ranch just one week later.

On an oath, he cut his truck right and skidded into
his long driveway, barely clearing the iron gates. Well,
he had everything now. With the help of one incredibly
loyal client who had believed in Jared's talent, he'd

become successful and highly respected in a short amount of time. The rich and famous came to him when they wanted to see and protect their financial future. Yes, he had it all.

Well, almost.

With his horrendous romantic history and intense work schedule, he didn't get involved with many women. But the ones he did understood that a few nights of enjoying each other's company was all he was willing to offer.

He was wealthy beyond his wildest imaginings, while Ben Thompson was now struggling to keep his ranch alive. That thought always made Jared smile.

The house that stood before Jared, however, made him frown. His three-story spread on four hundred acres sure as hell might be the symbol of his worth and how far he'd come, but every time he entered the gates and flew down the gravel road where his house loomed up before him, he was reminded of Ava. He'd had the house painted the color of her eyes—that soft, pale green. Lord, she had the kind of eyes a man could get lost in for days.

Jared ground his teeth, staring up at the place. When she'd left him four years ago, part of him had died. But the other part had remained alive to work. He'd worked his backside off night and day and dawn to get her out of his mind. Then later, to keep her out.

He'd created this place to look cheery and homey. And perhaps to his grandmother it was, but it sure wasn't to him. It was as though he'd built this house as an ode to Ava—in hopes that she'd come back, come home to him some day. But he'd been a fool, and the house had become just a place to rest his head at night.

He slammed on his brakes, skidding to a dust-cloud stop. He stared at the house, its white and Ava-green trim mocking him in the late afternoon sunlight. All he could think, see, was her. He cursed. All those years ago, Ben Thompson had made it clear that his daughters were off-limits to the ranch hands. Why the hell hadn't he listened?

Ben Thompson.

If it were the last thing Jared did it would be to get his revenge on that man. And if rumors of a financially troubled ranch were true, that looked to be soon enough.

"Are you going to get out of that truck?"

Jared glanced up at the porch where his elderly grandmother, Muna, sat at a small table surrounded by the things she loved. Tea, books, herbs of every kind and her spirit cards. She was his mother's mother and all he had left of a family. She was a true Cheyenne with salt and pepper braids stretching to her waist. She was thin, but far from frail. Eighty-four and sharp as a tack, she looked a bit wrinkled, a bit like a weathered apple—sweet but tart when she had a mind to be.

He remembered the stories she would tell him when he was a child. She'd been the shaman of her tribe, the one the people would go to for answers about dreams, visions and the future. She was called a "Teller" by some and a "Seer" by others.

Right now, Jared noticed, she was something else altogether. Apprehensive. She stood up and started to sweep the porch with long, swift stokes. "What happened in town, Jared?"

Inside his truck—which was growing warmer by the moment—Jared scrubbed a hand over his face. He didn't want to answer her question, so he chose a route more traveled: avoidance. "Why are you sweeping? We have a housekeeper."

"I didn't ask for her." It was her usual reply in her usual indignant tone.

Jared shook his head. All he wanted was for his grandmother to live the rest of her days in comfort. She and his mother had struggled all their lives, worked at any job that was willing to pay them a fair wage, just to put food on the table. And when his mother had died, it had been Muna who'd taken care of him. He'd just turned eight and he was a hellcat looking for trouble. But Muna had set him right, fed him, read to him—forced him to look past the cutting remarks and see that even a poor mixed blood could be someone. She'd been in her seventies while they'd lived on the Thompson's land and still found the energy to wash floors, cook meals and sweep porches.

Now, in her eighties, all she had to do was sit back, relax and enjoy life. But that wasn't her way.

"Jared," she called from the porch, her voice calm but laced with strength. "You better tell me what happened in town."

"I ran into an old…friend. Nothing to worry about."

She shook her head, unconvinced. "I felt something, but the cards were most secretive this morning. They didn't tell me about this old friend."

"Even the spirits of your animals couldn't have predicted this," he called, not moving from his truck.

She shrugged. "Maybe not. Or perhaps they wanted things revealed in their own time."

Four years was a helluva long time to wait for things to be revealed, Jared thought. Too long.

His only contact with Ava in all that time had been one phone call shortly after she'd left. But he hadn't

wanted to hear her excuses—hadn't wanted to hear
how she'd chosen another man over him.

He twisted the key in the ignition and gunned the
engine. Those days—those weak feelings—were gone.
He wasn't going to let any more time pass. Something
buried deep in his gut wouldn't allow him to just walk
away like *she* had four years ago, like he'd done in the
bridal shop today. It would've been different if he'd
never seen her again. But he had. She owed him an
explanation and once he had it, he could walk away
free. He could finally forget.

"I'll be back," he called to Muna as he shoved the
truck into Reverse. "I've got to see that old friend one
last time."

Jared barely heard the two-word utterance from his
grandmother that followed him on the breeze down the
gravel driveway. But he sure felt it—like a bullet in
the chest.

"Ava Thompson."

Two

In the dusky-blue guest bedroom of the modest house her sister rented, Ava stared out the window at her three-and-a-half-year-old daughter, Lily, who was laughing and playing in the backyard with the lively elderly woman from next door and her two grand-daughters. The three little girls were side by side, play-ing in the green plastic box Rita had filled with sand the day after they'd gotten there.

Ava felt her heart tug as she looked at her daughter. Lily loved the outdoors, loved to romp and play and make friends. But New York City wasn't built to ac-commodate a little girl with wide open spaces and a truckload of animals on her mind. Nor was it the best place to make friends.

In playgroup and out, her daughter had had a hard time of it. She was different, strong minded and pas-sionate. Someday soon, those wonderful characteristics would have her wondering who her daddy was—and *where* he was.

A fact which scared Ava, but she knew such a need was inevitable and that her daughter deserved to know the truth.

Lily's cheeks glowed with health and happiness as she played. Long auburn hair, almond-shaped eyes and a sweet face with an upturned nose and a sprinkling of freckles. In many ways she was a miniature version of her mother. But there was her father in her, too: dark-gray eyes that looked straight through to your soul, long legs and a fiery temper when she was frustrated.

On a weary sigh, Ava turned away from the window and grabbed the phone book off the top of the little white shabby-chic dresser. She needed to find a different place to stay—somewhere where there wasn't even the most remote possibility of Jared Redwolf stopping by.

"Hey. What are you doing?"

Ava glanced up to see her sister walk into the room, balancing a box of cookies under one arm and two glasses of milk in either hand. A still-shot flashed through her mind of a ten-year-old Rita bringing her cookies and milk on one of their mother's antique trays. As they grew up, Rita never tired of attempting to raise Ava's spirits when something went wrong, no matter if it was as minute as a put-down from their father, or as enormous as the horror in junior year when busty Tina White had flirted her way into the part of Laurie in their high school's production of *Oklahoma!*

What was especially amusing—and endearing—to Ava was that Rita still believed that cookies and milk were a cure-all for the blues.

Where Rita was the dreamer, impulsive and roman-

tic, Ava mused, smiling. She was the responsible one—
practical and cautious. To their mother's delight they
were truly characters.

Ava had always loved to hear the story about her
and Rita's names. Their mother, Olivia Thompson, had
been a stand-in for actresses Ava Gardner and Rita
Hayworth during a brief stint in Hollywood. One summer, she met Ben Thompson at a convention in Las
Vegas, fell head over heels in love with him and had
left all the glamour and her friends behind. But for her
mother, those days had never been never far away.
While she'd dress Rita and Ava up in old costumes and
powder their little noses, Olivia would tell them how
much she missed the Hollywood life and all the exciting people.

It was only a few years later that her mother had
died.

"So, who are you calling?" Rita asked, tugging Ava
back from the past.

"I'm calling all the motels in town."

Rita gasped. "You're not going to abandon me in
my hour of wedding need, are you? Besides, there's
only one motel in town now, and it's full up with rodeo
folk." She set the milk and cookies on the bedside
table. "'Course, there's Carolyn's Bed and Breakfast.
But Carolyn's not renting any rooms right now because
of the flood."

Ava's brow furrowed. "Her rooms are on the top
floor."

"Not from the rain." Rita popped a cookie into her
mouth and grinned. "Waterbed incident."

Ava put a hand up to stop Rita from saying anything
more. "Got it."

Rita reached out and took her sister's hand. "Please

don't leave. I'm sorry about today. I was a horrible sister.''

"Not horrible. Just exasperating, interfering and a devious little pain in the—"

"Okay, okay." Rita fell back onto the bed. "Look, I love you and I want to see you happy. What Dad did four years ago was so unbelievably wrong and unfair. I just thought maybe if you and Jared talked things over it would help the situation, maybe heal some old wounds.''

Ava smiled halfheartedly. "I appreciate that, little sister, I really do, but you saw how he looked at me today. The damage is done. It's over." She eyed her seriously. "And by the way, what Dad did wasn't your fault.''

A stain of pink brushed Rita's cheeks and she looked away. "I could've helped you."

"No, you couldn't have. You were too young." Ava sighed. "There was no painless way out of that situation. If I had gone to Jared, he and his grandmother would've been out on the street. Dad promised me that. And I wasn't going to let that happen."

"They have a big house now, you know." Her tone was leading and hopeful. "And no financial worries."

"I know," Ava said quietly, then pointed at the cookies. "Can I have one of those?"

Rita laughed and thrust the package toward her. "Have two." She sobered momentarily. "Are you going to see Dad while you're here?"

A flicker of apprehension coursed through Ava. "I don't think so."

"Maybe introduce him to his granddaughter?"

"He's made his feelings about Lily all too clear."

"He really changed when you left. Well, after his

car accident. That bump on the head seemed to knock some sense into him and some understanding into his heart. I think he'd really like to see you, Ava. I think he has some regrets.''

Ava shook her head firmly. "I can't take that chance. I won't have Lily hurt. I have enough to deal with in Jared.'' She nodded at the phone book. "That's why I should find another place to stay.''

"Oh, c'mon. He said he wasn't coming to the wedding, right?''

"Right.''

"So what are you worried about?''

Ava shrugged. Jared *had* promised not to come to the wedding, which meant he probably wasn't stopping by for an invitation. "I guess I really shouldn't be, huh?''

Companionably, they sat together on the bed, eating their cookies and drinking their milk.

Rita broke the silence. "He still has feelings for you.''

"Oh, I know. Hatred, contempt—''

"Whatever it is, you have to tell him the truth.''

"I tried once, remember?''

Rita put her arm around Ava. "You have to try again.''

"I just don't think he's ready yet.''

"*He's* not ready? Or you're not?''

Ava grabbed another cookie, stood up and walked over to the window to check on her daughter. She didn't even want to contemplate Rita's suggestion. Jared hated her now. And more than likely, after their exchange today, he wouldn't be coming within a mile of her—

The thought died. Ava's throat tightened and her hands began to tremble.

Through the thin pane of glass and dusty screen, a scene she'd imagined a thousand times in her head was unfolding. Lily had abandoned the sandbox and her friends and was standing beside the rosebushes talking to a tall, gorgeous Cheyenne.

"You got any horsies?"

Jared smiled down at the cute little girl with her large eyes and long copper ponytail. "Seven of them."

It was late afternoon, but the sun was so hot it could simmer chili. It was the kind of day that begged for water or shade. Or lemonade, he thought as the little girl sitting in front of him awkwardly handed him a Dixie cup from the kid-size plastic table that sat on the brick patio near the grass.

"Thank you, ma'am," he said and downed the cool, tart liquid.

He wondered who she was. Probably another one of Mrs. Young's grandkids—although she didn't look like one of those black-haired tikes. And if she was one of the Young kids, why was she over at Rita's place? Barbecue? Could be. Paradise was a real family kind of town.

He waved at a tired-looking Mrs. Young, then glanced down at the little girl who was tugging at his jeans. It was no spoiled, frilly-dressed young lady who looked up at him. No. The little girl who had intro- duced herself as Lily was dressed in jeans and a T-shirt, her cheeks and hands smudged with dirt. She was a tomboy, he could tell that the minute he'd walked into the backyard and she'd jumped up from the sandbox and leaped over the side like a circus performer—with no fear, only blind confidence. She had to be around three or four, but he wasn't sure. She wasn't totally forthcoming on that front, opting instead to pepper him with questions. Not that her pluck bothered him. He liked kids. Just didn't know many, that's all, didn't have much experience around them.

No brothers or sisters had meant no nieces or nephews.

Lily crooked her finger as though she had a big secret to share, and he bent down to hear her whisper, "My mommy reads me a book about Appaloosas." The word came out sounding like apple and ooosas. "You got Appaloosas?"

He nodded. "Two. Soon to be three."

"You might buy some more?"

"Nope." He sat back on his heels. "My mare's about ready to foal."

"What's that?"

"She's going to have a baby."

The little girl clasped her hands to together and let out a sound that resembled a squeal. "A baby?"

He chuckled. "Yep."

"When?"

"At the end of the week, I expect."

"Oh, I want to see. Please?" she asked. "I can help. I'm gonna be a good horsie rider when I get big."

A shadow fell between them on the grass. Jared stood and saw Ava walking toward the little girl, eyes wary and nervous.

"Mommy," Lily called to her with a wide smile. "This is Jared."

Mommy. Jared's gut constricted, making his breathing tight. This little girl was Ava's…child? The word cut deep, as did the idea that Ava had been touched by anyone but him. Although he knew she'd been married, he'd ripped the knowledge from his mind. Didn't want to think of her with another man. But here it was right in the face, proof-positive.

"I know who he is, Lil," Ava said at last, her green eyes fastened on him, questioning him. Why was he here and when was he going to leave? they seemed to ask.

About twenty minutes ago, he'd been tearing down Route 15, all fired up, ready to ask some questions, ready to do battle with the woman who held all the answers. But this little girl had stopped him, quelled his ire and charmed the socks off him as her mother had done so many times in the past.

Like Ava was doing right now, just standing there on the grass, watching him, her arms crossed protectively over her chest. He cursed silently as all thoughts in his head disintegrated while his gaze traveled over every inch of her. The pink satin potato sack she'd been wearing earlier was gone and in its place was the reminder of how luscious her body had been and still was. His groin tightened. White shorts, white T-shirt and chunky sandals. Long, tanned legs, high, full breasts and toes painted the color of his saddle.

Jared wanted only to be angry, feel the rage he'd been holding inside for so long, but this woman had a power over him. The sun pierced through the slats in the overhang like torrents of golden rain, backlighting Ava. Complete with a halo of blond locks, she looked like an angel. Too beautiful to behold. Well, too beautiful for *him* to hold.

Jared turned to Lily. "Your mom and I used to know each other."

Lily looked wide-eyed at her mother.

Ava smiled, then she glanced back at Jared. "Did you change your mind about coming to the wedding—"

"Not exactly." He eased off his Stetson and wiped his brow. This was not going as planned. One thing was certain, he thought as he looked at the two of them. He sure as hell wasn't going to interrogate Ava with her daughter around. It would have to be another time, another day.

Mother and daughter, he thought as he watched them sit down on the grass side by side, then start methodically picking blades of grass, discarding them. Why in the world hadn't he thought about the possibility of a child? What a fool he was. She'd left Paradise to get married. And children were a natural progression in a marriage.

"When can I come see the horsies?" Lily asked, forcing Jared back into the present.

Jared smiled. "You're welcome at my place anytime."

"Now?"

"No, Lil," Ava said quickly. "We're about to have dinner."

Undaunted, Lily said, "Tomorrow?"

Ava shook her head. "No. We…have plans."

She sounded utterly panicked, Jared noticed. Hell, she looked panicked. Obviously she didn't want him around her child. What did she think he was going to do?

His jaw tightened.

They'd talked about children once. The first night they'd made love. Late into the night in the small tack shed he'd fixed up to look romantic. They'd talked about everything: their future, being together, kids.

Then he'd pulled her close, kissed her hungrily and made love to her again. Jared shook the images of wet skin and heated mouths out of his head. He wasn't here to reminisce. She owed him an explanation and tomorrow would be the perfect time to get it. Muna could take Lily to see the horses and he and Ava could talk.

"What are we doing, Mommy?" Lily asked.

Ava startled. "When?"

"Tomorrow." Jared supplied dryly.

"Oh. Well, I thought I'd take you to the movies. That cartoon you wanted to see is playing."

"No," Lily said, her brows drawing together. "I wanna see Jared's horsies. One's gonna have a baby."

Ava tucked a stray hair behind Lily's ear. "Jared's a very busy man, sweetie."

In other words, Jared thought, she thought he should be leaving, getting back to that busy life and getting out of here. Fine, he'd give her what she wanted and be on his way. But not without a promise for tomorrow.

"I wanna help him with the baby horsie, Mommy."

"Oh, Lil. He doesn't do that himself. He hires a vet to—"

"Actually I do help in the birth," Jared interrupted.

Ava's brows rose considerably. "You do?"

"Don't sound so surprised," he said tightly. "I *am* good for more than asset allocation and stock portfolios. I was pretty handy on a ranch once upon a time."

Ava felt like crawling beneath the blades of grass that fluttered in the breeze under her hand. She hadn't said one sane word since she'd seen him and Lily together. She amended, "I know you are. I didn't mean that. I just never knew that you helped with foaling, that's all."

"There's a lot you don't know about me, Ava." He

jammed his hat back on his head. "And there's a lot I don't know about you."

The thin shelter of grass was far too open a place to hide, she thought. She scanned the ground, ashamed of those kinds of thoughts. She knew better than anyone that running away never solved a thing. Was she going to run forever? Was she ever going to stop, take a deep breath and face life?

Admittedly, facing life, past and future was partly why she'd come back to Paradise. She looked up into Jared's severe but magnetic gaze and found no shelter, no safe place to fall, only a deep yearning and seething anger.

At that moment, Lily jumped to her feet in a fit of spirit. "You can help us, too, Mommy."

"Listen, Lil, I never said—"

The little girl put her hands on her hips. "C'mon, peas?"

Saying no to the word "peas" was near to impossible.

"First things first," Jared said to Lily. "Why don't you two just come by tomorrow, then we'll see about helping with the foaling." He nodded at Ava. "My house at noon? Can't miss the place. Out the highway, then a right at Wes Lamb's place and down a few miles."

Ava opened her mouth to speak, then closed it as she shook her head. "I know you're really busy with your work. We can—"

"There's a lot to catch up on." He arched a brow at her. "I'll make the time."

"See, Mommy. He said he makes time."

Yes, he did, Ava thought, frustration setting in for the second time that day. She knew now that he wasn't here to get an invitation to Rita's wedding. He'd come here for answers. But Lily's presence, her existence, had thrown him, so he was pushing for tomorrow when he could get her alone. The thought unnerved Ava in ways she didn't want to explore.

"Can I pet the horsies, Jared?" Lily asked, her eyes dancing.

"I don't see why not." He gave her an easy smile. "It'll be good for them to see a pretty face after looking at the ranch hands' ugly mugs day in and day out."

Lily looked at her mother. "Mommy? Peas…"

Jared tipped his Stetson back. "Ava?"

It was a challenge—and one she knew she shouldn't back down from.

The unrelenting heat from the sun burned through her clothes. And no cool breeze was sent to rescue her. She felt herself nod. "All right."

Lily squealed. "I'm gonna tell Auntie Rita."

Yeah, tell Rita. She's going to love this.

"She's a great kid, Ava," Jared said as Lily took off into the house.

"Thank you." She gave him a tight-lipped smile.

"So, where's her father?"

She felt her smile fade. "Excuse me?"

"Your husband? Where is he?"

"As I said, we're not together anymore," she said quickly, coming to her feet.

A shadow passed over his eyes. "I can't help but wonder why you kept your last name." He looked up at her, his steely gray gaze searing through her. "Look, I was going to wait until tomorrow. But maybe we can get a head start." His brows raised expectantly. "Don't you think I've waited long enough to hear the truth?"

"The…truth," she fairly stuttered as she turned

away sharply, searching for the right words anywhere else but in his eyes.

She didn't get very far.

Her hand brushed against the picnic table, knocking over the pitcher of lemonade. She fought for her footing as ceramic crashed against brick, as liquid and ice spilled everywhere. Her pulse pounded in her ears. In an instant, she was on her knees grabbing for the shards of orange and green earthenware, Jared beside her.

Her mind churned at a hundred miles an hour. He wanted to hear the truth. But which truth?

Ava sucked in her breath and dropped a shard of broken pottery. Clutching her hand to her breast, she glanced down, her index finger stinging and aching. Tiny droplets of blood fell from her finger onto the ground and onto the jagged square of ceramic.

Jared reached for her hand. "You cut yourself."

"I'm fine," she said, pulling away from him. The last thing she needed was for him to touch her.

"Let me see it, Ava."

"No. It's nothing."

He took her hand anyway. Wasn't that just like him, she thought as she gave in to his strong, callused fingers, prying open her tight fist. A small gash marred her index finger. Nothing serious, just a bad scrape, but Jared was really focused on it. He grabbed one of the quickly melting ice cubes off the ground and placed it on the cut.

Ava sucked in her breath at the sharp pain.

"Sorry," he whispered, rolling the ice over the cut in small circles. "It isn't deep. No permanent damage done."

She glanced up at him, her traitorous gaze tracing the open collar of his shirt, then stopping to stare at

his smooth, tanned chest cut with pure corded muscle.
Her fingers twitched in remembrance of how his chest
felt beneath her hands, against her breasts. Beads of ice
water trickled down her wrist, begging her pulse to
slow.

"Ava, dinner's ready."

Rita called her from what seemed like a land far, far
away. But it was enough. Ava pulled her hand and her
gaze away from Jared and stood up.

He followed suit. "You should get some peroxide
on that."

She nodded.

"And I should go." He touched the brim of his hat
and started to walk away.

Last chance. To what? she thought. Run away, escape, try to get out of this neighborly call that wasn't
going to turn out very neighborly? She said, "Listen,
Jared, about tomorrow."

He turned and cut her a sideways glance. "What
about it?"

She bit her lip. This was getting ridiculous. There
was no escaping the inescapable. He deserved the truth.
Hell, he demanded it. And whatever happened tomorrow she'd deal with it—here or back in New York. At
least she and Jared could be free of a four-year burden.
She took a deep breath, praying that he was ready to
hear what she had to say. "We'll be there at noon."

Three

She stood above him, unbuttoning her blouse at the pace of a lazy river tumbling over smooth stones. Wrapped in the gentle light of a crescent moon, she locked her gaze with his and bared one creamy shoulder, then the other. A smile tugged at her full lips as she dropped her arms to her sides, allowing the silky fabric to fall to the grass beside her bare feet.

Even the cool grass beneath him couldn't quell the searing heat that shot straight to his groin. He was hard and waiting. He was always hard and waiting when she looked at him that way: determined and far past hungry.

A sudden breeze moved past, catching her hair, blowing it about her face. Her nipples beaded beneath the sheer, pale-pink bra she wore. She was beautiful, and he couldn't stop his gaze from traveling lower to her smooth abdomen, downward to what other sur-

prises awaited him. His throat went dry as he witnessed the shadow between her thighs. It was heaven barely masked by the slip of pink at her hips.

"Say it, Jared," she whispered, lowering herself on top of him.

He chuckled, cupped her buttocks firmly and whispered, "Happy birthday, Ava," against her neck as he rolled them sideways.

She lay beneath him, her sweet scent intoxicating— like honey and wildflowers.

"I want your mouth," she said.

Slowly, agonizingly slowly, he lowered his head to within inches of hers, their mouths a breath away. She ran her tongue over her lower lip and arched her hips up to him, her eyes pooling desire.

He cupped her face in his hands, ready to take what was his, what he'd been waiting for for years—maybe all of his life.

Suddenly her eyes clouded over. "Jared. I… I have to—"

He kissed the tip of her nose. "You don't have to do anything, sweetheart, but relax and enjoy."

Her gaze flickered to his mouth, then returned to his eyes as though she were pondering his offer. Then her hands found his face, her fingers found his hair and he groaned, leaning into her palms. "Ava. I love when you touch me."

"Jared, I have to go," she breathed, her hands continuing to caress him.

He felt himself nod. "Later."

"Now." Her voice was insistent, but calm.

Through foggy eyes, he tried to focus. "What's wrong, sweetheart?"

"I don't love you. I've never loved you." Unrelent-

ingly she raked her fingers through his hair, held him tight and moved beneath him. "There's someone else."

"No," he practically growled.

She offered him a teasing smirk before she leaned in and whispered in his ear, "You're such a fool, Jared Redwolf."

Jared sat bolt upright, the morning sun assaulting his eyes, his senses, his mind. Tangled in sheets and drenched in sweat, he fought for air—he fought to make sense of what had just happened. His gaze darted right and left. He was in his bed, fists clenched, jaw tight. What the hell? He looked at the clock: 7:30 a.m.

It was back. He rubbed a hand over his face, groaning at that dreaded realization. He hadn't had that dream in three years. That damn dream that had always had his body aching for Ava, while his mind, his tongue longed to curse her.

Take it easy, Redwolf, he urged. She'll be gone in a few weeks. Out of your life and your dreams for good.

But what about his mind? he wondered, knifing a hand through his mussed hair. Would there ever be a time when she wasn't in his thoughts?

He glanced at the clock once again: 7:33. If today went as planned, that hope was possible. And with a little help from Tina Marie Waters tonight, it might even be probable. The sexy redhead was always around, and any time he visited her she'd always ask him to stay late, stay until morning. He'd never stayed before, but maybe he'd just take her up on that offer. Hell, rules were made to be broken. Especially in dire circumstances.

And Ava Thompson was a dire circumstance.

He shut his eyes for a moment only to see her im-

print on his mind, standing above him in those pale-
pink strips of lace, her skin like satin and her eyes
flashing velvet-green desire.

"Dammit!" He opened his eyes, ripped off the bed-
covers and jerked out of bed.

After today, she'd be a distant and forgettable memory even if that meant he'd never sleep again.

"I think carrots were the perfect choice." Ava took
her daughter's hand as they left Killer Chicken Market
and stepped out into the sunshine. "If you were a horse
what would be your favorite treat?"

"Bubba gum ice cream," Lily replied without a moment's hesitation.

Always decisive, Ava mused as she followed her
daughter's example and jumped over the cracks in the
wide sidewalk that paralleled Main Street. Where Lily
had learned such superstitious behavior was anyone's
guess, but the skipping and jumping and laughing was
all good in Ava's book. She liked to play with her
daughter. She hadn't allowed herself much of an easy-
going childhood and Lily was a good teacher. The
games definitely took some of the levelheadedness out
of Ava, replacing it with a carefree heart. Of course,
today, she'd have to skip a good fifty miles to acquire
a light heart.

In about a half hour, they were going to see Jared
and his horses. Well, Lily was anyway. Ava was just
tagging along. And she hated to admit it, but seeing
his house, the life he'd made for himself, was a tempting prospect. While seeing *him* was just plain tempting.
Even if it came with a hefty price tag: telling him the
truth.

"Don't let go of my hand, sweetie," Ava reminded Lily as they walked across the street.

"Mommy, how come nobody honks horns here?"

Ava laughed. "I guess they're not in a very big hurry." She looked around, the coolness of a Bigtooth Maple tree overhead giving her a moments respite from the hot sun. "It is pretty quiet compared to Manhattan, isn't it?"

Lily nodded. "I like it here."

Ava stopped in front of her car and looked down at her daughter. Really looked, deeply. "Do you, sweetie?"

Lily nodded again, her large, gray eyes bursting with wishes and wants.

The windows to the soul really were just that, and Ava wondered if someone looked deeply enough into *her* eyes would they see that she wasn't happy in New York, either. That it wasn't her home and never would be.

She turned away from her daughter and unlocked the car door. In just a few weeks they had to go back to New York whether they wanted to or not. They'd made a life there, some semblance of a home. Heck, she had a great job and clients who depended on her. She didn't really belong here.

"That old man's staring, Mommy."

Lily's words pulled Ava out of the fog that held her mind captive and she glanced up. For a moment she could only stare back at the old man across the street that Lily was pointing to, her pulse racing. She hadn't seen him in four years, but it felt like longer. He hadn't changed much, but the lines etched in his face were deep and weighty. She cursed herself for wondering what made him look so unhappy—for caring at all after what he'd put her through.

"What's wrong, Mommy?"

Ava gripped her daughter's hand, feeling excessively protective. "Nothing, Lil. Let's go."

Let's get out of here before I say something or he says something or—

"Ava?"

Too late.

She stopped where she stood—trying to urge her daughter into the car—and turned to face him. "Hello, Dad."

Family, and friends of the family, had always kidded with Ben and Olivia Thompson that neither one of their daughters looked anything like either one of them. Two blond kids born to two brunette parents. Ava was certain that she'd inherited a few of her mother's features, but none of her father's. Not until today anyway. There it was, plain as day. Not a feature exactly, but an expression—one he'd never worn before—and it surprised her. Doubt and hesitance. She'd seen that very same look a thousand times in the mirror.

He gave her a tentative smile. "You're home."

She only nodded. Her throat felt constricted.

"It's good to see you." He dropped his gaze to the little girl at her side. "Is this Lily?"

Ava nodded, gripping her daughter's hand. "Yes."

Please don't say anything cruel, she begged silently as she watched him lower onto one knee in front of Lily, his body making all those crunches and cracks that came with age.

"Hi, there," he said.

"Hi." Lily moved closer to Ava. "Who are you?"

Ava held her breath, her hand fisting around the car keys.

"I'm your grandpa."

Lily smiled and gave him a nonchalant shrug. "Okay."

Relief spread like a warm blanket over and through Ava, but it was swiftly replaced by fear. Fear of her daughter knowing her grandfather and someday being rejected by him. When love was tossed aside in favor of pride, people got hurt. Very hurt. She didn't trust the man making nice to her daughter.

"It's my birthday," Lily was telling him, holding up six fingers. "In this many months."

He smiled. "I know."

She giggled. "You do?"

Of course he did. A time that, to Ben Thompson, would most assuredly live in infamy. Next he'd be asking her what she'd like for a present, Ava thought as she tugged on her daughter's hand. "We have to go, Dad. We're expected somewhere."

"I get to see the horsies at Jared's house," Lily supplied. "Do you know Jared?"

Ben Thompson came to his feet, the lines around his mouth tightening. "I do."

Ava turned away, darkness surging through her. He hadn't changed at all. He was still a sad old bigot. What was she thinking standing here? It was as if she was waiting to be hurt by him again. She opened the back door. "Get in the car, Lil."

Lily paused, then shrugged. "Bye, Grampa."

"Goodbye, Lily." He smiled at the little girl, then followed Ava around to the other side of her car. "Could you come by the house sometime?"

She didn't look at him. "We don't have much free time."

"How about a quick dinner? You and Rita and Lily."

Ava tried to swallow the grapefruit in her throat. Why was he doing this? Why was he playing nice now? What did he want?

"Thursday?"

She found his gaze.

"'Round six?" His eyes were hopeful.

She looked over at Lily. The little girl was smiling brightly in her car seat. Looking hopeful, too. With the lack of men in her life, of course she sought out a father, a grandpa—of course she was hopeful. But Ava just couldn't allow that hopeful, sweet face to turn sad and tearstained when her grandfather finally rejected her the way Ava knew he would. She wouldn't allow her daughter to get hurt, ever.

"I'm sorry," she said quietly but firmly as she climbed into driver's side of the car. "I don't think so."

She left him standing there as she pulled away from the curb, her heart tugging with the pains of the past. Lily didn't say much, just looked out the window—and honestly, Ava was thankful.

Minutes later, she was headed down the highway toward Jared's place, wondering why she felt so guilty.

Because you're holding on to secrets and past hurts that need to be set free, she chided herself.

She barely saw the road, barely heard the country music spilling from the radio or Lily singing along. Coming home was like facing every fear she'd ever had. And today would be the most difficult—facing Jared. In his home.

She smiled, her mind drifting backward. Long ago, in her little bedroom facing the barn, she'd sat on her window seat and watched him, back against the barn door with a lantern beside him, working on prospectuses, drafting letters to clients, studying the markets. So controlled, so serious when he needed to be—but patient when the situation called for it. At those moments, she'd imagined him coming home to her in their house, kissing her hello. It sure wouldn't have been a peck on the lips. No sir. Not even when they'd been married for twenty years. It would've been a ten-minute affair at the door, her back to the wall, his knee pressed in between her quivering thighs.

A balmy breeze rushed through the car window, assailing her as though it were determined to make her warmer still. As if that were possible when she was already thinking of Jared, she mused, slowing the car and turning right at Wes Lamb's place.

In spite of herself and the bumpiness of the gravel road, she returned to her childish fantasies of Mr. and Mrs. Redwolf. Back to that very thorough kissing session at the front door and afterward when she'd take his hand and steer him into the dining room. He'd eat two helpings of her home-cooked dinner, all the while telling her how delicious it was—and how delicious she was, he'd add with a devilish wink. Then they'd proceed to the bedroom, if they could keep their hands off each other for that long, to work on the big family they both wanted.

Ava glanced in the rearview mirror at her daughter and smiled a little sadly. Brothers and sisters for Lily.

"Look, Mommy."

Ava stopped the car directly in front of a driveway. A very, very long driveway with two enormous iron gates. One stood open, one remained closed—emblazoned with a bronze R in the center. R for Redwolf. Her palms felt damp against the steering wheel. Just the heat, she assured herself.

She'd heard that Jared had done well for himself, that he had a large home with acres of land to call his own. But, Ava mused, as she pulled into the driveway and whizzed past the bronze R, this was far past doing well. The land on either side of them was vast and lush and evidently prosperous.

"Look, horsies," Lily called, pointing to three chestnut beauties grazing in the distance.

"Wonderful, aren't they?" Ava said. "Which one would you ride?"

"All of 'em." Lily giggled. "Like at the circus."

They continued to chatter about the little things that made up country life as Ava drove slowly up the long gravel driveway. But a stunned silence overcame them both when they pulled into the circular driveway and beheld one of the most beautiful houses they'd ever seen.

Sheltered between two imposing oaks stood a three story sage-green farmhouse with white trim and a gabled roof. Red and purple flowers decorated the deep planters that were bordered by taller plants and shrubs, while window boxes filled with masculine-looking plants in shades of rust and amber decorated every other window. But the house's true glory was its wraparound porch. It was massive, matched the white trim and housed a swing for two. The columns that held up the porch's roof were intricately carved with signs and symbols that Ava recognized as Cheyenne, but she didn't have any idea what they said or represented.

As she stepped out of the car, she noticed those re-

markable Cheyenne baskets that she'd come to love so
much gracing the steps that led to the house. Each was
filled with herbs and strawberry plants. Then she noticed the woman who made those beautiful baskets de-
scending the steps herself.

"Haahe," she greeted them in Cheyenne as she
moved toward Ava with the grace of a gazelle. "It's
so wonderful to see you."

"Hello, Muna." Tears welled in Ava's throat as the
old woman gathered her up in her arms and squeezed
tightly.

"Jared!" Lily shouted, car door slamming. She ran
toward him, up the steps and embraced him around the
legs. She said with great enthusiasm, "I got carrots."

Ava glanced up and saw him, master of the house,
handsome as hell, standing just outside the front door.
And then he made a heart-wrenching move; he picked
up her child.

With worn jeans, a white T-shirt and work boots, he
was dressed like a typical Texas cowboy, although he
was anything but. He was long, lean and oozed authority, his black hair pulled off his strong, angular
face—that sun-bronzed face where piercing eyes
dwelled.

Be still my heart, Ava thought as she walked beside
Muna toward him.

Jared watched Lily with the horses, amazed at how
fearless and full of life the little girl was. "She's a
natural, Ava."

Ava smiled. "Thanks for letting her come today."

"I'm happy to have her."

He and Ava stood side by side at the barn door,
watching Muna show Lily how to brush down the very

pregnant Appaloosa. The horse was tied to a hitching ring attached to the outside of her stall in the wide aisle that ran down the center of the barn, looking amazingly calm. At first Jared had been wary about letting the little girl get too close to the horse. Tayka had been a bit skittish lately, not wanting too many people around her. But as soon as Lily had offered her a carrot, stroking the broad white blaze that ran from Tayka's forelock to her velvety nose, the horse had seemed to fall under the child's spell.

"Look at Tayka," Jared whispered to Ava. "How calm she is. I've never seen her act this way with anyone."

"Lily loves animals. She'd spend every moment with them if she could."

Why wouldn't she look at him? he wondered, taking in her ironing-board posture and tense jaw. "She has a gift, Ava. It's a shame that you live in a big city. She should be around animals more often."

"I'd love to give her that," she said, still watching Lily, a hitch in her voice.

"But?" he prompted, curious.

She turned to face him then. "New York is our home."

"And you want her to be close to her father?"

The tension hung between them like a velvet curtain. Her eyes darkened as she bit her lip. "Something like that."

Jared turned around and leaned back against the barn door. He was saying far too much, getting far too friendly. However much he liked Lily, she was the daughter of a woman he wasn't going to see ever again after today. Like Ava herself, kids simply weren't in his future. Not that he hadn't always wanted a couple—

or three or four. But you had to get married to raise children properly. And marriage wasn't in his plans. Kids deserved two parents that loved them and each other.

Jared's hands balled into fists. If he ever did become a father, he'd make damn sure to be a good one. Not like his own father. The man who had abandoned him and his mother the minute he'd found out she was pregnant.

But since he wasn't willing to start anything that lasted more than a month, the making of a family was likely to happen. And it was just as well. He wasn't going down that road again. He liked being single.

Muna rose from her little stool beside Lily. "I think it's time to fix our guests some lunch, Jared."

"No, thank you, Muna," Ava said quickly. "Lil, we should really get going. We'll stop at the diner for something."

Jared laid a hand on her arm and felt her shiver beneath it. "You like bologna and cheese, Lily?"

The little girl nodded enthusiastically. "My favorite."

He turned to Ava, leaving his hand on her arm, trying not to notice how soft her skin was—trying not to remember all the other places she was just as soft. "Why don't we go up to the house and make some sandwiches?"

Ava threw him an anxious glance and eased her arm away.

"Go ahead you two," Muna called. "I'll stay with Lily."

Ava looked as though she were trying to appear calm. "Are you sure, Muna?"

Jared glanced over at her sharply, knowing that she

was afraid to be alone with him and wondering what she was thinking. He reined in the anger and frustration at all that had changed since they'd held each other in the dark and whispered words of love all those years ago.

Muna nodded at Ava, her eyes shining. "I'm very sure. We are having fun." She winked at Lily. "Yes, Little Star?"

The little girl grinned from ear to ear.

"All right," Ava acquiesced. "Just be careful. We'll be back soon."

Little Star? Jared mused as he and Ava walked up the hill toward the house. It had been Muna's name for him when he was small and he wondered why she would call Ava's child something so dear and familiar.

"Your place is beautiful, Jared," Ava said as he held the front door open for her.

Small talk. He could deal with small talk for now. "Thanks. I'm proud of it."

"You should be." She glanced up at him as she brushed past him. "And of yourself for creating it."

He smiled at that, inexplicably pleased by her praise. "Kitchen's through there." Why'd she have to look so pretty? So enticing with her blond curls piled on top of her head, showing off her long neck? He couldn't help but stare. Her legs stretched on for days in those tan shorts she wore. And that shirt—pale pink and formfitting. Had she seen his dream, too? Known that that color would drive him mad, make him break out into a sweat, perhaps cause him to forget why he'd invited her here?

It was odd, but he'd never let any woman but Muna journey past the foyer of his house. Why did he have to break that practice now, and with this woman?

He watched her as she stopped to admire the table
his grandfather had carved so many years ago. She ran
a hand over the smooth surface, pausing at the tiny
crack Jared had accidentally inflicted on it when he was
six years old.

As much as he didn't want her to be in his house,
to see his things, he felt the need to explain the table's
wound. "I used this table as a military headquarters
when I was a kid. Trucks, men, big, sharp rocks, tanks.
I loved playing army. With all the wear, I'm surprised
there's just a little scratch."

Ava watched his expression turn childlike as he de-
scribed the scene. She never thought she'd miss him
so much just being with him, but she did. She said
softly, "I remember you telling me that. You liked to
beat up men and pick on poor defenseless women,
right?"

"I've never known a defenseless woman."

"I was one."

He rolled his eyes. "Yeah, right."

On a chuckle, Ava moved to give him a playful sock
on the arm. But Jared was too quick for her, nabbing
her wrist and pulling her tight against him so she
couldn't move. He asked, "Are you going to behave?"

Breathing seemed impossible as she stared up at him,
into those dark eyes, but she managed a faint, "Are
you?"

He pulled her closer. "I don't know. Do you want
me to?"

Ava's mind dotted with memories—being this near
to him. That moonless summer night when they went
swimming in the lake just outside of town, nude, their
bodies pressed against each other, legs entwined, lips
desperate…

Perhaps he heard her mind's silent call, perhaps not—but before she could answer he pulled away.

"Yeah, I really messed up that table," he said, his tone calm, his gaze black. "But all kids do stupid things, right? I bet your dad has a story or two about you and Rita."

She smiled awkwardly, trying to ignore the heat riding waves through her body. "More like five or six." Her gaze fell. "I should have asked him to give me a few when I saw him today. Then you wouldn't have been the only one sharing past foibles."

He inhaled deeply, remarked, "So, how is the man? I hear his ranch is in trouble."

Rita had mentioned something along those lines, but Ava hadn't wanted to hear the details. That place held so many memories, good and bad. "I don't know what's going to happen to the ranch or what my father's going to do. I haven't seen or talked to him since I left Paradise—until today, that is."

Jared's gaze snapped to hers in surprise. "You haven't spoken to your father in four years?"

"No, I haven't." She looked away. "We should get those sandwiches. Lily gets cranky if her stomach's empty for too long."

Though his mind and gut yearned for answers, Jared decided not to press her. Besides, her feelings about her father shouldn't be any of his business. But as he led her into the kitchen, questions burned in his mind. Why hadn't she talked to him in all that time? She couldn't possibly know what Ben had done to him after she'd left. God knows, Ben wouldn't have offered the information.

And why was she acting so nervous? Had New York City changed her so much? Or was it the husband?

Hell, he wanted to know everything that had happened to her, starting with the last night he'd seen her. But when he noticed her standing in the center of his kitchen, his brain temporarily shut down. She was looking around the room, her hands on her hips, her back arched, her breasts jutting out. The same need that had rose up to claim him back in the dining room sprung up to claim him once again. What would have happened if he'd actually kissed her like he'd wanted to? he wondered.

"So what can I do?" she asked him.

Now that was a question, he thought darkly. When he'd first moved in here, how many times had he thought about the two of them stretched out on the cool red tiles beneath his feet? His groin tightened painfully. What an idiot.

"The bologna and cheese are in the fridge," he said, forcing an impassive tone into his voice. "I'll get the bread."

"I've never seen a kitchen like this." She walked up to the large, Sub-Zero refrigerator. "Fireplace, comfy chairs and a large, family-style table. It's so impressive and well...homey."

"Not what you expected, huh?"

"No."

Jared relied on the only emotion that could quell his desire for her: cynicism. "Surprised the mixed blood's not still living in the back of your father's barn?"

She shut the refrigerator door and turned to face him. "Why would you say something like that? I compliment you and you turn it into something ugly. Is this just about being angry? Are you trying to misunderstand me?"

He tossed the loaf of bread on the counter oh-so

casually. "I think our misunderstanding started a long time ago. The day you left without a word."

"So this *is* about anger." She fiddled with the twist tie on the bread, not opening it. "You knew where I was, Jared. You didn't exactly come running after me."

"I don't chase women who don't want to be caught."

"And I don't beg men to follow me."

He opened the package of bologna. "A simple good-bye would've been enough."

She looked away for a moment, then back. "I'm surprised you even missed me."

She would never know how much. "Don't worry about that, darlin'. I got over it pretty quick. Surest way to forget one woman is to find another."

Her eyes went wide, and she looked as though he'd just slapped her. "Is that why you didn't take my call that night? Because you were entertaining a woman?"

He hadn't taken her call that night, one year to the day after she'd left, because it would've killed him. He forced a hard smile to his lips. "I wouldn't exactly call it entertaining."

Two bright red spots colored her cheeks. "I should go."

"You're not running away again, dammit!"

"Fine," she shouted at him. "Why don't you just say what you need to say and let's end this?"

He felt his anger wash through him as he crossed the room in four easy strides. Standing directly in front of her, he said, "I want the whole truth."

"I can't tell you everything, Jared. And what I can say probably won't satisfy you."

"I'm not looking for you to satisfy me." He gritted

his teeth. She was the only woman who had ever truly satisfied him. Why the hell did she have to be the one who infuriated him the most as well? He felt the heat rushing off her body, but didn't give in to its power. "I want to know why you didn't come to me all those years ago, why you didn't at least let me know you were leaving?"

She shook her head. "I'm sorry. I couldn't."

"That's no answer."

They were so close he could see the tiny gold flecks in her troubled green eyes, smell the floral perfume that she'd worn since high school. He cursed under his breath. Why did he want to shake her and kiss her at the same time?

"I... I had to leave, Jared. My father didn't give me any choice."

"You're going to blame this on your father?"

"No. I blame myself, but I'm trying to explain the circumstances."

He raked a hand through his hair. "What could the circumstances possibly have been? I thought we had something."

She touched his arm. "We did."

"You just had something more with that guy in New York."

She dropped her hand. "No."

"Dammit, Ava. Then what was it?" He shook his head. "What was so important that you could leave like that?"

"I had to go... I was afraid if I didn't—"

"Mommy?" Lily called from the other room.

Breath held, Ava just stared at him. "Jared—"

"This is far from over," he whispered.

"Mommy?"

Ava nodded at him, then called out to her daughter, "I'm here, Lil."

The little girl appeared at the door, Muna beside her.

The older woman looked from Jared to Ava. "She wanted to show you both something out in the pasture."

"Jared has a pony," Lily said happily. "I walked him round the…the…" She looked over at Muna.

"The corral, Little Star."

Ava smiled down at her. "That's wonderful, Lil."

"You're on your way to becoming a real horsewoman," Jared said, his voice softening along with the rest of him.

The little girl's eyes grew wide. "I am?"

He nodded as Ava went over to her and took her hand. "We have to go, honey. I have a fitting at Mrs. Benton's in half an hour. I'll get you something at the diner."

"I'm not so hungry. I ate carrots and Muna gave me bread with corn in it." Lily gave Muna a big hug, then ran to Jared.

He hugged the little girl tightly, feeling altogether too melancholy that they were leaving. "Did you have fun today?"

She pushed away from him and smiled, nodding enthusiastically.

After everyone had said their goodbyes, Jared followed Ava and Lily out to the driveway, watching as Ava got into the car with her daughter. He stared after them, a renewed feeling of loss sweeping over him as they took off down the driveway in a flurry of dust.

Maybe it was better just to leave things as they were, he thought as their car disappeared from view. She was never going to give him what he needed to hear—that she hadn't loved him—that there was nothing between them, then or now.

"She has become a beautiful woman." Muna came to stand beside him on the edge of the gravel driveway.

"Yes."

"Her daughter is very much like her."

He nodded.

"But she has her father's eyes."

Surprised, he turned to look at the old woman. How in the hell would she know something like—

"Truth is hidden in the heart, but seen in the eyes." She touched his face gently. "You don't see what's right in front of you?"

"What are you talking about?"

"Lily is your child, Jared."

Four

Ava lifted her face to the cool shower spray and sighed. *Nope. Still sweating. Maybe I should switch it to cold.*

It was close to ten o'clock at night and excessively warm. Rita's air-conditioning was on the fritz, but that wasn't the only thing that was keeping Ava's temperature high. She knew she was also suffering the after-effects of being in Jared's presence today—as well as in the unsettling enclosure of his arms.

Within the confines of the royal-blue shower curtain, a fine mist held in the air around her, while above her, beads of water pelted her face and neck as if she were a flower in a summer storm.

And damn, if she wasn't close to wilting.

How could so many things happen in one day? she wondered wearily, letting her head fall to her chest, allowing the water to cascade down her back. Today,

she'd seen and talked to her father and he'd met Lily.
He'd invited them to the house with a look of what
Ava could only describe as tenderness on his weary
face, and he'd treated his granddaughter with respect.
A surprising set of events. No, shocking was more like
it. Rita had told Ava he'd changed. But to what degree,
she wasn't sure. And did she even believe it? Did she
even want to believe it?

One thing she *was* sure of, involving herself and Lily
in a new relationship with Ben Thompson would be a
risk.

Ava slashed a hand across her wet face. She just
wanted the pain in her heart to fade away. Pain she'd
received as her heritage from her father, pain she'd
passed on to Jared who'd loved her.

Jared.

Her Cheyenne warrior. The man to whom she'd
given her love and her virginity so many moons ago.
Today, he'd stood beside her at the barn door watching
Lily with the horses. A serene atmosphere. But she
could sense that his mood was far from calm.

But neither was hers, if truth be told. She had en-
countered such feeling later that day when he'd almost
kissed her. Curse her weak soul. She'd wanted him to
kiss her. She'd melted against him, wanting to taste
him again and again. But Jared had quickly released
her, perhaps remembering why she was there, and began to fire questions at her, demanding answers she'd
been too cowardly to give him.

Ava turned and let the jets pound her neck and back.
Tomorrow morning she would return to Jared's ranch
and tell him the truth once and for all.

Fear coursed through her at the thought, but she

willed it away. She would stand her ground with him and take what was coming to her.

Grabbing the bar of lavender-scented soap from the wall caddy, she worked lather between her palms then began to soap herself. Her legs and hips, then upward to her stomach and breasts. In her mind's eye she saw Jared, his black hair loose and splayed across her smooth chest, his mouth on her breast, his tongue laving her nipple. An ache deep in her core—one that had been imprisoned far too long—awoke with a husky cry.

She moved the soap higher to somewhere safe and tried to will those sensuous thoughts away. But they didn't obey. They returned full throttle. She saw her body entwined with Jared's—one dark and one light—heavy with sweat on a bed of hay in an abandoned stall. Would she ever be able to rid that night from her mind? Would she ever be able to be with another man and not see Jared's face? Or would she forever see his smoky-gray eyes fixed on hers as she rode the waves of pleasure?

Ava closed her eyes and breathed in the scent of lavender. But this time, the soap's mild fragrance did little to calm her and she put it back in its niche and rinsed off.

Obviously it wasn't just the deceptions of the past that had her trembling. It wasn't just the heat that had her feeling things she hadn't felt in four years—things she never thought she'd feel again. It was Jared, and the way he looked at her when their eyes locked and their lips were a mere breath away. Being close to him was like standing near a volcano. Consciously, you knew it wasn't erupting, but you always felt as though it could at any time.

And if it did, you knew you'd be lost in its heat forever.

Taking a deep breath, she turned off the water and stepped out of the shower. Hoping for a cool breeze to rush in from the open window, she was disappointed, but not surprised, at the humid puff of air that barely made contact with her sensitive skin.

She quickly towel-dried her hair and slipped on her comfy powder-blue robe.

Bed. Sleep. No two words had ever sounded so good, she mused, as she walked down the hall to her room quietly so she wouldn't wake Lily. Ava cracked a smile as she opened her bedroom door. Waking up Lily would be close to impossible after such an exciting day.

From the center of her room came a *click,* then warm yellow light assaulted her eyes and filled the small space. Ava gasped, her gaze scanning the room as a sudden breeze blew through her window. Pulse racing, she could only stare. Jared Redwolf sat on the over-stuffed chair by her bed, his arms crossed over his chest and a scowl that would make a grown man quake in his boots fixed on his lips.

"No more running away, Ava."

Jared's voice was like ice, his eyes hooded and dangerous. Ava felt as if her breath was slowly being cut off. She wanted to run, but she stood her ground.

"What…what are you doing in here?" she stuttered, glancing over her shoulder before closing the door behind her.

His eyes narrowed as if inspecting her. "Muna mentioned something interesting to me after you left."

"Did she?" Ava asked a little weakly.

He nodded. "Something about me—and Lily."

Ava's stomach dipped. "Lily…"

"Can you guess what it was?"

Ava bit her lip. Yes, she could guess. Quite easily, in fact. Muna…the Seer. Ava's pulse quickened. Was it possible that the older woman had seen too much?

"Can you guess, Ava?" he asked again, this time with husky force.

With a small laugh, Ava said stupidly, "Was it how you both love horses?"

Jared sniffed. "No. Something far more personal. Something that brought me all the way out here. Something that had me climbing up that naked, rotting tree out there and into your room."

He knew. Or at the very least suspected. "We could talk this over tomorrow," she said lamely. "I'll come to the house."

Jared didn't move, just stared at her.

Ava's hands started to tremble and she shoved them into the pockets of her robe. "It's late. Rita's right below us and Lily's just a few doors down."

His gaze pierced her very soul as he said in a dangerous tone, "Muna said she thought Lily looked like her father."

Ava felt the color drain from her face. She wasn't ready for this. The look on his face, the guilt in her heart, the foolish hope that he might forgive her and want them both in his life again still hovering inside her.

"Eyes like her father, is what she said," Jared continued, his own eyes blazing steel fire under the arched brow he shot at her. "What do you think?"

"Jared, I…"

A muscle flicked in his jaw. "Is Lily my child?"

Her breathing grew shallow and she took an involuntary step back.

His lips thinned. "So help me, Ava, if you try to skirt around this—"

"I won't. I'm not." She closed her eyes and shook her head, her wet hair slapping against her face. "This is not how I wanted to tell you."

"Looks to me like you weren't planning on telling me at all." His tone went black as night. "Say it, Ava."

She pulled her robe closer around her. "Yes." Her voice was only a notch above a whisper. "She's yours, Jared."

He muttered an oath. Then another. Then he stood up and walked over to the window. "Lily…"

Silence filled the room. Tension filled the air as Jared stared out the window and Ava stared after him, her heart aching with regret, with thoughts of what could have been if she'd had the guts to stand up to her father.

"That little girl." Jared's voice broke with emotion. "That sweet, feisty little girl with copper hair and gray eyes is mine?"

Ava's eyes filled with tears. "Yes."

He turned back to face her and she'd hoped his eyes would be tender still thinking of his daughter, but his face was a mask of rage. "Do you have any idea what you've done?"

Ava stiffened, his ire pulsating through her. "I was only trying to protect her—"

"Protect her from what?" he demanded.

"Don't look at me like that, Jared."

"From the big, bad, filthy half breed who was too

poor to provide for you and yours, too worthless to
make it off your father's ranch?''

She shook her head, said vehemently, ''No!''

''You didn't come to me and tell me you were pregnant because you thought I couldn't support you and
Lily.'' His voice was low and overflowing with contempt.

She stared at him, her heart hammering against her
ribs, her mind searching for the right words. But nothing was coming. Only the truth. But telling Jared the
truth, telling him that her father was ready to toss him
and Muna out of their home, would only serve to con-
firm his belief that she didn't think he could provide
for a family. Her stomach twisted into knots. She didn't
want that. She didn't want him to hate her—hate his
daughter's mother.

''What about the guy?'' he asked.

''What guy?''

''Your husband, Ava.'' Jared crossed the room in
seconds, stood inches from her. ''Did he know?''

Did he know? She wanted to laugh, perhaps with a
touch of hysterics. There was no husband. In fact,
there'd never been anyone but Jared in her life. No one
but Jared in her bed. But she couldn't say so, could
she? To Jared, another man was the reason she'd left.

She closed her eyes momentarily, needing to grasp
hold of her bearings. Clearly she and Jared were over,
and the threat her father had placed on him and Muna
was past history. What difference would telling him
about her lack of husband make now? The most important thing was Lily. Her little girl deserved the father she'd been wanting for so long and Ava was going
to do everything in her power to make sure that happened. Whatever it took.

When Ava opened her eyes again, Jared was staring at her, waiting for an answer.

"My husband knew about Lily," she said, feeling ashamed with every word she uttered.

"So you only lied to one of us, then?" he muttered.

"Jared, I'm so sorry. I was young and scared. I didn't think—"

"You sure as hell didn't think." He scrubbed a hand over his face, and the anger in his eyes was gradually replaced with misery. "You had no faith in me, Ava. You couldn't see that someday I was going to make good—that if you stood by me for just a little while, you would've had everything you ever wanted." The small scar at his temple twitched, his eyes narrowed as he regarded her suspiciously. "But you see that now, don't you? Did you really just come back here for your sister's wedding?"

She went cold. "What do you mean?"

"I'm no poor ranch hand, now, darlin'," he drawled with heavy sarcasm.

"Jared, you're talking crazy—"

"Here's what's crazy." His tone was low, menacing. "You know what you've done, Ava? You've turned me into my father. With everything I've done in my life to be different from him, you've managed to turn me into that worthless good-for-nothing sperm donor who wanted nothing to do with his child."

The words hit Ava in the gut and she lowered her gaze, shame fisting her heart. She knew Jared's history, his vow to create a different kind of life than the one he was given and the pain he had from a father who'd left him and his mother.

Jared was watching her, his eyes softening for a moment. "Why didn't you tell me, Ava?"

"I tried."

"Once. You tried once."

Guilt jabbed at her. He was right. She had tried once. And when he'd rebuffed her, she'd slunk away. His slight had been enough for her. She'd wanted to forget Paradise, her father, the love of the man she thought she could never have and who had obviously moved on with his life and into the bed of another.

"I'm so sorry," she began, her vulnerable side appealing to his. "I wanted to tell you. I swear it."

But he'd already returned to resentment. "You swear it? That's funny. Do you think I'd believe anything you say now?"

"Jared, you and I need to—"

"There's no you and I." He brushed past her and walked to the door, his boots clicking on the hardwood floors. It was a sound she'd once embraced. Long ago, it had meant he was coming to her. Tonight, it meant he was leaving.

"Listen well, darlin'," he said coldly. "I'm not going to let you keep me from my child ever again."

Her chest tight, Ava turned and watched him walk out the door, closing it softly and carefully behind him. Even in his anger, he was thinking about his sleeping child in the next room. He would have been a wonderful father, but she'd never given him the chance. Fear had guided her every movement and she'd have to live with that for the rest of her life.

Was he right? she wondered, wandering over to the bed and collapsing atop the cool sheets. Had she followed her father's orders because she hadn't believed that Jared was capable of taking care of her and Lily and Muna?

No. No. She was trying to protect them all.

Tears of anger and frustration welled in her throat. Her sister had never understood her motivation for leaving Paradise, and now it was obvious that Jared wouldn't, either.

Fear gripped her as she thought about his last words to her and the punch of revenge in his voice. What had he meant about keeping Lily from him? He wouldn't actually try to take her daughter away, would he?

A hot tear rolled down Ava's cheek as she hugged her pillow to her chest. She'd only allowed herself to cry once in the past four years. She was long overdue.

Astride his favorite Appaloosa, Jared rode hell-bent for leather across the plains and skidded to a stop just above Ben Thompson's sprawling ranch, a place now weathered and worn from lack of care. It was late, close to two in the morning and Jared couldn't sleep. He'd tried to bury his nose in work. He'd even tried burning sage in his sweat lodge. Nothing had worked. The words spoken between he and Ava tonight—the acknowledgment that Lily was his flesh and blood—it was too much for a man to hold in his mind without air and open sky.

He had a child.

God, the thought gripped him to the core.

A beautiful, sweet baby that he'd never seen until yesterday. It was wondrous news, yet his anger at her mother attempted to slay his joy.

How could Ava have kept something like this from him? How! Her ridiculous mumblings about protecting the child… It was ludicrous.

Tomorrow he would call a private detective friend of his and see about protecting himself this time. He didn't want Ava bolting again, taking Lily with her.

And then there was the ex-husband to consider. Jared needed to find out where the man was and if he had any claim on Lily.

In the meantime, he thought gazing down at Ben Thompson's poorly neglected ranch, he'd be careful about pressing Ava. She might get scared and bolt again and he couldn't risk that. He wanted to be with his daughter too much to risk that.

Under the starry sky and massive full moon, Jared's gaze caught on the roof of the tack shed he'd spent so much time in, preparing for his future.

The small shed was also the place where he'd met her, where he'd made love to her—where he'd gone after her father had told him foully to pack up his grandmother and his tomahawk and get the hell off his land.

Beneath Jared, his horse snorted as if he'd heard the racial slur in his master's mind. Obviously Ben had known that his daughter carried a mixed blood's child and couldn't stand having Jared on his property. It all made sense.

And now that property was in financial trouble, Jared mused with a sinful grin. Well, he'd wanted to pay Ben Thompson back for some time, hadn't he? And that need had never carried such a feeling of desperation as it did now.

Yes, he thought, turning his horse around and crying out into the black night for the Appaloosa to run home, seeing that man, that place and all its old memories destroyed might just satisfy his taste for revenge once and for all.

The afternoon sunlight followed Lily as she skipped along the lakeshore, the pale yellow beams pausing

with her as she spied a particularly shiny rock and
stopped to scoop it up. With a gleeful cheer, she
grabbed it, tossed it as far into the water as she could,
then whipped around to smile at her mother and her
aunt Rita.

From the grassy hill just above the water, two sisters
sat side by side—Rita waving, Ava smiling with pride
at the little girl she'd raised all by herself. Her sweet,
sassy daughter.

Hers and Jared's.

Ava pulled her bare legs to her chest and rested her
chin on her knees. Last night was still very much on
her mind. Guilt at her cowardly past and fear of what
Jared was planning to do in the near future had haunted
her through the wee hours. But she felt stronger today.
And very protective. Of course, she wanted Lily to
have a relationship with Jared. But she wasn't going to
let anyone take her daughter from her. Even her daughter's father.

Beside her, Rita laughed as she watched Lily follow
a bullfrog, hunched over, leaping forward with her
hands and feet and making "ribbet" noises.

Starring Lake was working its magic, Ava mused,
grabbing some suntan lotion from her bag. It almost
made her forget her own set of troubles. More like an
ocean's cove than a lake, Starring could make even the
shallowest spirits soar. Hidden by rock and brush and
virtually unpopulated, it took hard work to hike up the
rocky hill and maneuver your way down through the
tall brush to the lake's shore.

But it was worth it.

Paradise within Paradise, Jared used to call it. A perfect circle of blue, a beautiful valley of water surrounded by flower-dotted hillside. No boats could get

in or out, so there was no pollution and plenty of wild-life. Years ago, they had found this place together and it had been their refuge, an oasis where no one could find them.

"It's been three hours, sis," Rita said, prying Ava from her thoughts. "I don't think he's coming."

Ava nodded. After breakfast that morning, she'd called Jared. She'd wanted to ask him to meet her, to talk, see what they could work out. But no one had been home.

"Maybe he hasn't gotten the message," her sister suggested.

"Maybe he did," Ava said glumly.

Rita took a sip of orange soda. "You could go to *him*."

"I thought of that, but I don't want to descend on him unwelcome and unannounced. I thought this would be the perfect place. Calm, no people—he could see Lily."

"He's angry, Ava."

"I know and I don't begrudge him that." She chewed her lower lip thoughtfully. "I'm just afraid of what he might do."

"He's a good man, Ava. He needs some time to let it all sink in. Becoming a father overnight is a major deal."

"I know." Ava started cleaning up the remnants of their picnic. They had gobbled up all their lunch and played a dozen games. It was time to go home. But Lily didn't look ready to go, she thought, watching the little girl with the frog she'd finally managed to corner. Lily wanted to play in the water and go fishing. She liked to look at all the tall plants and tiny water crea-tures that swam amongst them. Anyone could see that in the little girl's mind, Paradise was already becoming familiar and favored. Ava couldn't help but wonder how she was going to get Lily back on that plane to New York.

"Ava, look." Rita gestured toward the hillside, her voice eager.

It was him. Ava's pulse skittered alarmingly. She slipped on a pair of shorts over her bikini bottoms and watched as he walked down the hill toward them wearing the kind of jeans that spoke volumes about his maleness. Faded, fitted and rough. Without his Stetson, his hair hung loose to his shoulders, its dark color glossy against his black T-shirt.

He looked dark and dangerous and she wished right then and there that he still belonged to her.

She watched as Lily raced toward him, all innocence and adoration. Jared scooped her up and held her, his eyes closing, his ruggedly handsome face etched with sadness and longing. The picture of them together sent a flash of grief rippling through Ava. How many times had she dreamed of such a sight? A hundred? A thousand?

After many long moments, Jared put Lily down, said something to her, then pointed to where Ava sat. The little girl nodded and scampered back to the lakeside and her frog.

Rita touched Ava's hand. "I'm going to take my niece for a swim. You going to be all right?"

I don't know. But to Rita she uttered a firm, "Fine," and gave her a half smile, then watched her walk down the little path toward the lake, passing Jared with a quick, "Hello," on the way.

Jared gave Rita a nod, but he offered no greeting to

Ava as he approached, just sat down next to her and said resolutely, "I want to see Lily."

"And I want you to," Ava answered, her anxiety threatening to steal her breath.

"Every day."

"Okay."

His jaw tight, Jared clipped her a nod. "Bring her by the ranch around noon tomorrow for a visit."

He wasn't going to take Lily, she thought. He wanted to know her, spend time with her, but he wasn't going to try and take her from her mother. Relief poured through Ava like a glass of ice tea on a hot day and she told him brightly, "We'll be there."

Jared cut her a sideways glance, his expression cool. Then his gaze flickered downward, his jaw tightening as he roamed the length of her. Bare legs, black shorts, exposed midriff, and black bikini top. Ava felt her cheeks warm as he paused at the gentle slope of her breasts, which tingled beneath his gaze, their peaks just visible through the thin fabric of her bathing suit top.

He thrust a hand through his hair and looked away. "*We'll* be there," he repeated tightly. "Don't trust me alone with Lily even now, is that it?"

"No, that's not it," Ava said gently. "Lily just won't understand why she's there if I don't come along."

"Well, then, let's tell her the truth."

Ava grabbed his arm. "No!" It was such a violent outburst, she almost frightened herself.

"Why the hell not?"

"I don't want to upset her."

He shot her another contemptuous look. "More like you don't want her to be upset with you. You don't want her to know that her mother kept her away from her father.''

At such bitter truth, tears huddled in Ava's throat. ''Maybe not.''

Jared stared at her, then his gaze fell once again to her breasts. He cursed and looked away. ''Couldn't you have worn something decent?''

''We're at the lake, Jared,'' she said with a stiff sounding chuckle. Though secretively, she was glad she still affected him. It was all she had left. And Lord knew he still affected her something awful. ''You're right about me not wanting my daughter to be angry with me, but I'm trying not to base my judgments on that fear.''

He turned to face her once again, but didn't respond.

''Jared, I just think that you should let her get to know you. Let her feel comfortable and secure around you before we tell her.'' Again, he said nothing and she added quietly, ''But maybe you're too angry with me to see that.''

His brows slanted gravely. ''I'd never hurt my child.''

She tried to smile. ''I know you wouldn't. How about if we decide when it's best to tell her.''

''Together?''

She nodded. ''Together.''

He nodded, then started to stand up.

Ava couldn't stop herself. She grabbed his arm and said without thinking, ''I'm glad you know the truth, Jared. So many times I wanted to—''

He cut her off with a simmering look. ''Let's make something clear. I'm not going to forgive you for what you've done. My only interest is in Lily.'' He stood up and walked away, walked down the hillside toward the little girl playing at the water's edge in her bumblebee bathing suit. Spotting his descent, Lily waved and ran to him. He lifted her high in the air and she laughed.

Despair and happiness battled in Ava's heart as she watched the pair. But today she would concentrate on the latter, because today, her daughter had a father.

Five

Jared tightened the vise on the dowel with a little too much force. What was it they said? Hard work and sweat cooled the brain?

He took off his hat and wiped his brow. Well, whoever *they* were, they didn't know a thing. It was midday, inching up on ninety degrees and he didn't feel cool inside or out. Anger still gripped him. His temper flared every time he thought about how Ava had deceived him. How she'd robbed him of four years with his daughter.

He snatched up a piece of sandpaper and began to smooth the wooden rod of the stick horse he was crafting for Lily, the weight of his strokes cutting quickly through the grain. It was the first step toward making his present to her shine. He wanted her to know that this gift of wood represented the beginning. Hell, he wanted her to love it, love him.

Not surprisingly, he hadn't gotten a minute of sleep last night, and early in the morning he'd given up and headed down to the small workshop attached to the barn. Ideas for a present for his daughter had flickered through his mind, one after the other. A new swing set? A dollhouse? What would make her the happiest? She loved horses and wanted to learn to ride, he'd reminded himself.

Then he'd remembered how he'd learned to ride on a stick horse with handles coming out of its ears. The one his grandfather had made for his mother. Jared grinned. Some days it had felt as though he'd ridden all the way to Mexico on that horse.

It was one of the many things that had been left behind when he, his mother and Muna had moved from Oklahoma to Texas. When it had become obvious to his mother that his father was never going to show any interest in them.

Jared's smile turned a little sad as he remembered the brave face he'd put on when he'd spied the full car and the wooden playmate he'd had to leave behind.

The version he was making now wasn't nearly as grand or intricately carved, but it didn't matter. It was more important that Lily have something now, something from him, something of her own to play with.

"What's eating you, Redwolf?"

Jared glanced up and saw Tim Donahue, his burly ranch foreman, standing in the workshop doorway. From beneath his mop of graying blond hair, his brown eyes were curious.

"Nothing's eating me."

Tim chuckled. "Gotta be something. You look down in the mouth." He walked into the room and over to the workbench, ran a hand over the smooth wood pole. "Who's this for?"

Jared hesitated. He'd promised Ava that they wouldn't tell Lily he was her father until the time was right. But did that promise extend to others? he wondered. After all, Tim was a friend. And though he was a good twenty years older than Jared, he'd become something of a brother over the past four years. Someone Jared confided in. Hell, he knew the story of Ava leaving, and he knew that she was back in Paradise.

Jared rubbed a hand over his jaw. He wanted to tell Tim, but he just couldn't risk that information getting out no matter how trustworthy his friend had always proven himself to be. He needed to be sure that he was the one to tell his daughter the truth.

He gave Tim a neutral smile. "It's for a girl named Lily."

"Lily, huh?" Tim grinned widely, picking up a hammer and, without being asked, began to secure the leather straps for the stick horse's bridal with upholstery tacks. "This girl, she's what? Twenty-two?"

"Try three and a half."

Bewilderment marked Tim's sun-weathered face. "What are you doing hanging around three-year-olds?"

"I'm not hanging around—"

"Especially when Ava's back in town?"

The sound of her name startled Jared and his hand fisted around the handle of the vise. "I told you before, Donahue, Ava and I are history."

"Right. Right. So you did." Tim scratched his bearded jaw. "So then maybe this stick horse you're making is about getting in good with little Lily's mother, whoever she may be? Well, good for you."

Jared sighed with frustration. "Did you want something, Donahue? Or did you come in here to annoy me?"

Tim shrugged lightly. "I thought you might want some help, boss. That's all."

"Well, get to helping then."

On a chuckle, Tim held up the metal object. "I got a hammer in my hand, don't I?"

"I thought that was for me to crack you over the head with whenever you asked a stupid question," Jared replied.

Tim snorted. "Yeah, that's possible."

Brow raised in mock agitation, Jared said, "I'd be more than happy to prove it."

Tim shot back with a grin. "You and what five hands?"

Muna's laughter floated on the breeze behind them. "Always the same. Working side by side, bronzed backs, tall as oaks and wrangling like two bobcats over a deer."

Tim jumped over the head of the hobbyhorse and gave the old woman a peck on the cheek. "*Ne-tone to-mohta-he,* Muna?"

"I am well." She smiled. "*Hahoo,* Tim."

Jared grunted. "You don't need to thank him, Muna. Just don't teach him any more Cheyenne."

"Why not?"

"He uses it to pick up women." Jared scooped up the wooden horse's head and carried it outside.

"Where's the harm in that?" Muna asked, walking beside him.

Tim followed, his smile wide. "Yeah. What's wrong with that?"

"Pretending to be something you're not?" Jared felt

their light banter turn suddenly as he gently placed the horse down on the grass. Perhaps his mood, his experience with Ava was driving the conversation now. "It's lying, plain and simple."

Tim's brows shot together in an affronted frown. "You need to lighten up, boss." He broke into a chuckle. "Look, I give you my word, I won't use your language to seduce little Lily's mother."

"You've met Ava, then?" Muna asked Tim quickly.

Tim's eyes widened to the size of silver dollars. "So, Ava's Lily's mother, huh? I get it now." He grinned at Muna. "No, Muna darlin', I haven't had the pleasure of meeting Ava, but I've heard a lot about her."

Jared shot his friend one helluva an unfriendly glare, then took a mental step back. What was his problem? Why was he getting so irritated at Tim's innocent ribbing regarding a woman he no longer cared anything about?

As if on cue, Ava's rental car passed through the gates. Despite his previous thought, Jared felt the corners of his mouth turn up into a smile. There was Lily, sitting in the back seat, waving like crazy.

Tim eyed Jared. "Cute kid."

"Yep."

"And her mother, Ava. Beautiful name."

"She's a beautiful woman," Muna said, shielding her eyes from the sun.

Tim chuckled. "Is that so?"

"Don't you have somewhere to be?" Jared muttered.

"Nope."

Jared watched Ava pull into the driveway and park. Dammit, he was pleased to see them both. Not just his daughter, he realized with frustration, but both of them.

Well, maybe that was a good thing. He didn't want Lily to pick up on his anger at Ava. No. He would be cordial to her. Making them both as comfortable as possible.

Ava stepped out of the car with a tentative smile and jeans that looked so good they should be outlawed. Jared broke out into a whole new kind of sweat. The faded denim was molded to her toned legs and rounded hips, while her white tank top showed off every hill and valley she possessed.

As she walked toward them, Tim let out a long wolf whistle. Jared didn't have the time to slug the foreman because just then his daughter ran straight for him and propelled herself into his arms. She weighed less than one of his saddle blankets and her auburn hair smelled of sunshine. He held her above him, and she giggled delightfully.

"I'm all sweaty, Little Star," he said, using his grandmother's nickname for her.

"I don't care." She dropped down against his chest and squeezed him tight. "How's Tayka? Did she have her baby yet?"

"Nope, not yet." He held her a little away from him. "I promised I'd let you be here to see, don't you remember?"

She nodded, then caught sight of something behind him. Her eyes went wide. "What's that?"

Jared glanced over his shoulder. "It's a hobbyhorse. Your hobbyhorse."

"Mine? For my birthday?"

Jared froze. Her birthday. He had no idea that it was her birthday. His heart darkened with pain when he thought of how many birthdays he'd already missed. Anger surfaced again, gripping him, but he forced it back. Lily was still in his arms and he didn't want her to feel his tension.

"When's your birthday, sweetheart?" he asked the little girl he held in his arms and his heart.

"I'll be four in six months," she said proudly.

"Four already," he said with a teasing grin, relieved that he had so much time to plan for her big day.

"Look, Mommy," Lily called excitedly as Ava approached. Lily pointed to the stick horse. "It's a horsie for me!"

Ava smiled lovingly at her daughter. "It's beautiful, Lil."

"Come with me, Little Star," Muna said, holding out her hand. "We will take a closer look."

Lily wriggled out of Jared's arms and ran to Muna. Jared watched his child race over to the wood horse and embrace it, then he turned back to Ava.

Her gaze was fixed on Lily and the horse. "I didn't see that when we were here before. Where did it come from?"

"I made it."

Ava's gaze snapped to his. "Oh, Jared..." She touched his arm, then jerked her hand back. "It's beautiful. You did a wonderful job."

"Thanks," he said tightly. "I had some help."

Ava glanced over at Tim, who was hanging out behind Jared nudging an anthill with the tip of his boot. "I'm sorry for being so rude. I'm Ava Thompson." She blushed prettily, smiling at him. A bright, beautiful smile that made Jared's blood heat and something too close to jealously flare inside him. He looked over at Tim to see his reaction. His foreman was staring, entranced. Jared muttered an oath. He wanted to tell the guy that he'd better pick his jaw up off the ground before Jared did it for him. But Tim recovered from his ogling and stuck out his hand to Ava.

"Tim Donahue, ma'am."

"My foreman," Jared supplied dryly.

Ava smiled that killer smile again as she shook his hand. "It's nice to meet you, Tim."

"Likewise. I've heard a lot about you, and if you don't mind me saying so, Jared's description of you is dead on. You *are* as beautiful as a Texas sunset."

Ava blushed deeply this time, her gaze flickering in Jared's direction.

"You need to take yourself up out of here, Donahue," Jared growled. "Now."

Thankfully, Lily chose that moment to come running back into their awkward semicircle. "Can I ride the wood horsie, Jared? Please, please."

Jared looked at Ava and their eyes locked. Why the hell couldn't he move?

"I'll attach the rod and make sure everything's secure," Tim offered, a grin in his voice.

"Me and Mommy and Jared get to play all day," Lily told Tim as they walked away.

"Playing all day, huh?" Tim shot a long look at Ava over his shoulder before saying, "Sounds like fun."

Jared's lips thinned in anger. He didn't need his friend spurring him on with Ava. Tim knew all about his troubles with her—how long it took for him to get her out of his mind, out of his soul. Shoot, if Tim weren't such a dependable foreman, he'd be giving him the boot right after supper. Telling Ava what he'd said about how she looked! Hell. That was just plain low.

"You should go with them," Ava suggested, breaking the silence. "She's so excited for her day with you."

He nodded, feeling hesitant, but knowing he'd better remember that it was only Lily he wanted to spend time with. "Well, feel free to roam about the ranch or—"

"How about some iced tea, Ava?" Muna called coming toward them.

Ava gave Jared an almost relieved half smile. "Looks like I'm taken care of."

Jared watched her walk across the lawn, her hips swaying with the rhythm of the wind in the trees that lined his long drive. His groin tightened painfully and he turned away. He and Ava were separated again. But this time, it wasn't by evasion. It was by choice.

His choice.

Ava took a sip of her iced tea, then lifted her gaze and smiled across the kitchen table at Muna. "Mint and lemongrass. My favorite."

"I remember," Muna said, her eyes warm. "It wasn't so long ago."

A heaviness resided in Ava's chest as she said quietly, "It seems like forever."

"Ah… Being away from Paradise or from Jared?"

Ava grinned, shook her head. She couldn't help herself. That was the Muna she knew and loved and remembered. No beating around the bush, just straight talking—though her tough questions were always wrapped in affection.

"I've missed them both," Ava confessed. "One maybe more than the other."

Muna reached across the rugged oak table and covered Ava's pale hand with her brown, weathered one. "You are here now and that is what matters."

In that moment, as Ava looked into the eyes of the wise old woman before her, it was as if time had never passed and the solid connection between them had never been severed. Muna had always embodied the phrase, "welcoming arms." And for a girl who'd lost her mother early in life, Ava had cleaved to Muna, held tight to the aura of security, home and hearth that emanated from the woman. It had been unbelievably hard to leave Paradise without saying goodbye all those years ago, and Ava couldn't help but feel a new surge of guilt every time she looked at Muna.

She swallowed the lump in her throat and spoke from her heart. "I want to tell you how sorry I am for—"

Muna lifted her hand from Ava's and waved it about. "No, no. None of that now. You took the path that appeared the brightest—or appeared the least painful—I know. And perhaps it was. Perhaps it was not." A breeze wafted lazily through the large picture window to Muna's left, causing the stray hairs on her salt and pepper braids to dance. "Live now, in the moment, with no regrets, *Nahtona.*"

"*Nahtona?* What does it mean?"

Her mouth curved with fondness. "I will tell you another day, my dear."

It wasn't uncommon for Muna to plant seeds within a person, and Ava never pushed to have them watered. She much preferred to figure out how they grew on her own. So, she nodded her acquiescence and turned to gaze out the window. A smile tugged at her lips. Out on the sprawling lawn, amidst flowering plants and lovely shady trees, her daughter was running in circles astride her stick horse, holding the pole with one hand and the makeshift bridle with the other. Jared was calling out "Yee-ha" with a husky cry as Lily's long, copper hair flew about, her face emanating pure glee.

Suddenly all pleasure left Ava and she turned back to face Muna. "I have to say one thing."

"All right."

"I'm not proud of taking that path."

Muna smiled. "Then take another."

"I think I have." Her gaze flickered toward the window. "I hope I have."

"It's far easier to look back and point out the mistakes you've made than to see them at the time." She poured Ava another glass of the fragrant tea. "Your father knows this well."

"My father?" Ava said, surprised.

"He has also taken another path."

"Yes." She exhaled heavily. "Rita told me that, too. I don't know if I can ever believe it, though."

"Why do we fight against forgiveness?" Muna seemed to be asking no one in particular. Then she looked up and smiled. "Thank you for bringing Lily to meet her father. And her great-grandmother."

"I hadn't exactly planned...well, Rita's wedding was really the—"

Muna's smile broadened. "It was time for all of you to know your truths."

Ava flinched at her words. If Muna only knew that there were still deceptions to be had, she thought. Her fictitious husband and the real reason why she'd left Paradise. Those truths hovered in the air around Ava like a swarm of troublesome mosquitoes.

"Shall I read your cards?" Muna asked her.

The warmth of the kitchen turned oppressive. No matter how interested she was in what was to come, Ava didn't think Muna's cards would be able to enlighten her at all. Her future was not predicable at this

point. It was up in the air with those tiresome mosquitoes.

"Not today, Muna, but thank you."

The old woman just nodded, a faraway look in her
eyes.

Jared saw Ava glance down at her watch for the
second time in a half hour. It was dark outside, close
to eight-thirty and cooler than usual. He didn't want
Ava and Lily to leave, but he knew they probably
should. His first real day with his daughter had been
one of the best of his life, and later when Ava had
joined them out on the grass, lying back, watching the
clouds pass across the sky, it had been damn near perfect.

Muna had prepared a wonderful dinner and afterward Jared had built a fire in the living room where
the four of them sat close to the hearth and traded jokes
and posed riddles. They'd all forgotten about the past
in those few hours, especially when Muna had spun
one of her stories about her life on the reservation as
a young woman. Riveted, Lily had sat at her great-
grandmother's feet, drinking in every word.

Until about ten minutes ago that is, Jared mused,
taking in the little girl's closed eyes and peaceful expression, her head resting in her mother's lap.

They should go, Jared told himself silently. This was
not a family no matter how much it felt like one. And
the sooner he got that through his thick head the better.

He watched Ava gather Lily into her arms. He
couldn't help thinking about Lily as a baby, lying on
Ava's chest, cuddling, cooing, nursing. He had missed
so much.

Ava caught his eye, whispered, "I need to get her home."

"She could stay." The words were out of his mouth before he could stop them. "I have a room for her."

Ava lowered her gaze.

"And for you, too," he added, not sure how he was going to react in the hours between bedtime and dawn knowing she was only doors away.

Stay away from her, Redwolf. She's out of your life. Only Lily matters, only Lily is important.

"I don't think so," Ava began. "It's a strange house and—"

"She's asleep." Muna rose from her place beside the fire and walked to Ava, touched her shoulder. "Let her stay."

Ava looked up at Muna, gave her a soft smile. "All right."

Muna nodded. "Very good. I have baskets to finish. Good night Ava, Jared." She bent, kissed Lily's flushed cheek. "Good night, Little Star."

Fast asleep, Lily didn't stir. Jared heard the soft footfall of his grandmother ascending the stairs as he glanced over at Ava. The light from the fire made her beautiful face glow, made her blond hair alive with the colors of a tigress. Warning sirens blasted in his head. He'd assumed that Muna would show Ava to her room, but now he was alone with her, faced with the unnerving task of taking her upstairs and showing her where she was going to sleep.

He mentally shook his head to scatter the unwanted images that dwelled there. "Let me put my little girl to bed, Ava," he said. "Afterward, I'll show you where you're going to sleep."

Her gaze searched his, then she nodded. "Okay."

He knelt beside Ava and slid his arms beneath his daughter. For one brief moment, they were all touching, all connected, and he'd never felt a pull so strong. Ava's soft perfume crept into his nostrils and took up residence. Why did she have to still wear that scent? he wondered dumbly, his pulse thundering in his blood. And why hadn't their physical attraction died—or even subsided—in four years? Even now, when he knew she'd lied to him, kept him from his daughter, he still wanted her.

Their gazes caught, held them both captive. Only the unrelenting sounds of the ticking wall clock, the snap of the fire and Lily's deep, peaceful breathing could be heard.

Finally Ava looked away and released Lily into his arms. "I think I'll see if the kitchen needs some attention. We didn't let Muna out of our sight after dinner."

"I'm sure it's done. We have a housekeeper."

"Really? I didn't see her today."

He hugged Lily tighter and whispered, "She stays out of Muna's way. I hired the woman to help so Muna wouldn't have to work anymore, but my stubborn grandmother was far more insulted than grateful."

Ava chuckled softly. "Lily's stubborn when she wants to do something herself. She must've gotten it from her great-grandmother."

Ava paled and awkwardness sat between them for a moment. Her eyes held sadness and perhaps a little shame, for she'd kept Lily from her great-grandmother, too. But her shame and his anger couldn't be helped now. What was done was done, and Jared needed to keep the peace for his daughter's sake.

"Why don't you come up with us?" he suggested. "Like you said, it's a strange house, strange bed."

She shook her head. "I'll stay down here for a while. I want you to have this time with her."

Why the hell did he want to say, "Ava, it's *our* time to be with *our* daughter?" That wasn't how it was going to work—or how he wanted it. Sure, they were going to share Lily. But in different houses, different holidays and very separate lives.

He nodded, said, "If you change your mind, it's upstairs, second room on the right," then started up the stairs.

"Oh, wait a sec," she whispered behind him.

He turned to see her rifling through her big blue duffel bag. She pulled out several things, then held up a book.

"She always wakes up a little when I put her into bed. She likes to be read, too." She met him on the third stair and handed him the book. *The Giving Tree.* "It's her favorite."

Stars, brilliant diamonds against black velvet, dotted the night sky. From the spacious balcony attached to her room, Ava leaned against the railing and looked over Jared's vast property. The cool air felt heavenly against her skin and she closed her eyes and breathed in the scents of hay and roses.

She smiled as she recalled her phone conversation with Rita a moment ago. Ava hadn't expected a lecture from her sister about spending the night at Jared's, but she sure hadn't bargained on the five-minute cheerleading session that concluded with the phrase, "Now I know it's been a long time, so if I can answer any questions…"

"Do you need anything else?"

Ava turned sharply to find Jared stepping out onto

the adjoining balcony. Her breath caught. So their rooms were next to each other, were they? Was this a wise idea on his part?

Fifteen minutes earlier he'd seemed completely different—softer—as she'd watched him from the doorway of Lily's room, taking a seat at the edge of her little girl's bed and breaking out *The Giving Tree*.

Right now, however, he looked imposing standing there in his sweatshirt, jeans and bare feet, practically taking up the entire space. The soft lights behind him cast his tall, well-built form in a hazy glow. He was truly the sexiest man alive and he was sleeping right next door.

Four years ago she would have been standing beside him, touching him freely, kissing that full mouth whenever she wanted. But now…

"Pillows, extra blanket?" he said, running a hand through his thick black hair.

Another thing she could've done any time she'd wanted to, she thought. "No, I'm fine. We'll be out of your hair in the morning." She felt her eyes widen at the slip. "Thanks for the…hospitality."

He crossed his arms over his chest, leaned back against the railing. "You make me sound like a Holiday Inn."

"In that case, I'd like the key to the mini bar."

"Having a Milky Way craving?"

She cracked a smile. "I'm desperate." She shook her head, laughed softly. "I can't believe you still remember that."

He pushed away from the wall, grinned. "Those cravings were serious. No Milky Way, no kiss. No kiss, no—"

He came to an abrupt halt, plunged both hands into the pockets of his jeans.

Ava felt her skin warm, though a cool breeze continually blew. She mused on the private memories that had been locked away in her heart until now. Every night a Milky Way had appeared on her nightstand. And on those nights when she could sneak out to meet him, she gave him a long thank you. Afterward, they'd share the candy. Once he'd even sneaked the candy bar into the hospital when she'd broken her wrist.

"Look, I've been thinking," Jared began. "Anger between parents is no good for a child. I'm willing to be civil if you are."

At that moment she'd be anything he wanted her to be. She swallowed hard. "Civility works for me."

His gaze suddenly caught on the left side of her face. He walked to the very edge of the balcony. "Don't move." He reached out for her, his hand brushing past her face and into her hair.

She practically sighed and melted against his palm.

He pulled back, a pretty white moth in between his thumb and forefinger. He lightly tossed it into the air, then his compelling and bone-meltingly seductive gaze found Ava's. "Trapped in Paradise."

She held her breath. No truer words were ever spoken.

His gaze moved downward and his eyes turned black as coal. With great calm and coolness, he turned and walked away, back into his bedroom, calling over his shoulder, "Good night, Ava."

She stared after him, thanking whoever was listening above, beyond those perfect stars, that Jared had said good night, not goodbye.

Six

Ava lay on top of him, her hair pulled back off of her face, her eyes imploring him as her naked body pressed against him.

"Jared..."

She whispered his name, her lips moving in slow motion, her hands raking his shoulders and up his neck.

"Jared, please."

When she asked like that, he could deny her nothing. Quick as a cat, he rolled over, slipping her beneath him. He was hard as granite and ready to bury himself deep within her.

"Jared! Wake up!"

His eyes flew open, his heart pounding like a jack-hammer. Shafts of sunlight coated the walls of his room like burnished yellow paint and Ava lay under him, her frame molded to his, her hands cupping his face. For a moment he thought he was still dreaming, but that wasn't possible. Ava was fully dressed now and her eyes weren't filled with the desire of a moment ago. They were a deep forest-green and highly agitated.

"What are you doing here?" he said, his voice husky with sleep, husky with lust.

"What am I—" She shot him a withering glance. "You grabbed me and pinned me under you."

"Not under me, dammit! What are you doing in my room?"

"Lily's sick, Jared," she said, attempting to wriggle out from under him. "I think she has a fever."

He was off of her in seconds. "What?"

"It might've been something she ate yesterday," Ava said, coming to her feet. "Her stomach hurts and—"

She stopped talking and her gaze dropped, then widened. Jared glanced down and quickly realized that he was highly aroused and not wearing a stitch of clothing. Cursing, he yanked the sheet off the bed and covered himself.

Ava's cheeks flashed bright red. "I would have gone to Muna, but I didn't know where her room was."

"Why would you go to Muna?" he said tightly. "I'm Lily's father. You come to me."

"I did come to you, and you practically..." She gestured toward the bed.

"I was asleep, Ava. I didn't know what the hell I was doing." He raised a brow at her. "Can you turn around for a minute?"

With a heavy sigh, she did as he asked. "Look, I was going to go to Muna first because I thought she might know where I could find a thermometer. Do you have one?"

"I don't know. Doubt it." Jared pulled on his jeans, a knot the size of boulder forming in his gut. His child was sick and he probably didn't even have something as standard as a thermometer. "Well, I'm not going to waste time looking for one."

"What do you mean?"

"I'm calling a doctor."

"I thought of that, but it's too early," she said over her shoulder. "They won't be in."

"This isn't the big city, Ava. Doc Ward's a friend. He'll be here in ten minutes." He tossed on a T-shirt. "You go back to Lily. I'll be there in a minute."

She turned to face him. "Jared?"

"What?"

"Don't sound so worried. Every child gets a little stomach bug from time to time. It's normal."

"Is it?" His jaw tightened. "I wouldn't know."

He watched her expression turn from sympathetic to weary, and felt a twinge of regret. With a short nod, she left the room.

Jared snatched up the phone. Why should he feel guilty for saying the truth—for getting angry? He had a sick kid in his house and no experience under his belt. He felt totally inept at being a father. Totally insecure about his role.

What if Lily needed his help and he had no clue how to help her?

Tightness settled around his chest.

He didn't know a damn thing about being a parent, he thought, punching in Doc Ward's phone number. And the one person that did, the person who could teach him—help him become a good father—made him angry as hell and crazy with lust.

* * *

"She needs plenty of fluids and lots of bed rest. But she should be up and about in a couple of days."

Ava looked across the coffee table at the doctor. The balding man with friendly eyes and a soft smile had given Lily a thorough check-up and had declared her stomach pains and slight fever a mild case of the flu. Just as she'd thought. But Jared had needed the doctor's analysis. The doctor must have been a pretty close friend, too, someone to be trusted, Ava mused, because Jared had told him the truth about she and Lily, then sworn him to secrecy.

Ava glanced over her shoulder at Jared, who had refused to sit down and was standing, arms crossed, behind the couch. With all of the doctor's assurances, Jared still looked worried, and for the first time in a long time, Ava felt thoroughly connected to him. She knew that anxious, out-of-control feeling so well. It was a shame that she couldn't talk with him about it, offer him a little comfort.

"So, besides the children's Tylenol and rest and fluids, there's nothing I can do?" Jared gripped the back of the couch and eyed the doctor. "Are you sure we shouldn't have some tests done or—"

Impulsively Ava reached back and put her hand over his. Almost immediately, he captured her fingers beneath his callused palm and began to stroke the top of her hand with his thumb.

Ava swallowed hard, her pulse picking up speed. She'd meant to calm him with the gesture, but instead his intimate, incredibly arousing caress was only succeeding in making *her* agitated. She slipped her hand from beneath his, though it took great mental and physical effort to do so.

Jared hardly noticed. "Maybe there's some kind of herb, Doc? Muna knows—"

"It's just a virus, Jared," the doctor assured him, standing up, grabbing his black bag. "Give her the Tylenol every four hours and make sure she gets plenty of sleep. You have my word. She'll be running around like a jackrabbit in three days."

"I'll bundle her up really well before I take her back to my sister's house, Doctor," Ava promised, giving the man a thankful smile.

"She'll stay where she is," Jared declared rather loudly, stepping out from the back of the couch and to the doctor's side.

"Jared, wait a minute—" Ava began.

He shot her look so fierce, she practically gasped. "I will be with my daughter."

Frowning, Ava shook her head. "But the flu is contagious. You and Muna —"

"Do you have to move her, Ava?" the doctor interjected. "It might be best—"

"No, she doesn't have to move her. Lily will stay here." Jared's tone was low and determined as he stared at her, daring her to break the law he'd just decreed. The doorbell rang and he gestured toward the hall. "That'll be Rita. I called and told her to bring over some things for you and Lily."

"You did what?" Ava shot to her feet, thoughts spinning in her head, anger stirring in her blood. "Would you excuse us for a moment, Doctor?"

Doc Ward smiled sagely and nodded. "Of course."

Ava grabbed Jared's hand and led him out of the room and into the hall. Once in private, she whirled on him. "I understand you're master of your domain here,

The Silhouette Reader Service™ — Here's how it works:

If offer card is missing write to: The Silhouette Reader Service, 3010 Walden Ave., P.O. Box 1867, Buffalo, NY 14240-1867

NO POSTAGE
NECESSARY
IF MAILED
IN THE
UNITED STATES

BUSINESS REPLY MAIL
FIRST-CLASS MAIL   PERMIT NO. 717-003   BUFFALO, NY

POSTAGE WILL BE PAID BY ADDRESSEE

SILHOUETTE READER SERVICE
3010 WALDEN AVE
PO BOX 1867
BUFFALO NY 14240-9952

Play the Lucky Hearts Game

and get...

2 FREE BOOKS
and a **FREE MYSTERY GIFT...**

yes! YOURS to KEEP!

I have scratched off the silver card. Please send me my *2 FREE BOOKS* and *FREE mystery GIFT*. I understand that I am under no obligation to purchase any books as explained on the back of this card.

Scratch Here!

then look below to see what your cards get you... 2 Free Books & a Free Mystery Gift!

▼ DETACH AND MAIL CARD TODAY! ▼

© 2002 HARLEQUIN ENTERPRISES LTD.
® and TM are trademarks owned by Harlequin Enterprises Ltd.

326 SDL DZ5S

225 SDL DZ57

FIRST NAME

LAST NAME

ADDRESS

APT.#

CITY

STATE/PROV.

ZIP/POSTAL CODE

(S-D-05/04)

Twenty-one gets you
2 FREE BOOKS
and a **FREE MYSTERY GIFT!**

Twenty gets you
2 FREE BOOKS!

Nineteen gets you
1 FREE BOOK!

TRY AGAIN!

Offer limited to one per household and not valid to current Silhouette Desire® subscribers. All orders subject to approval.

but you're not my master. You don't get to make decisions for me or my—''

He raised a brow at her, his eyes a deep, burning gray.

She put her hands on her hips. "Decisions about our daughter should be made by both of us.''

He took a step forward, closing the distance between them. "You've made every choice regarding Lily's welfare for the past four years.'' His eyes bored into her. "I think you can grant me some leeway here.''

Ava could barely catch her breath. One inch closer and they would be touching, the tips of her breasts to his hard, smooth chest. "Jared, we can't stay in this house.''

"*You* can't stay in this house, you mean.''

"How would it look?''

"I don't give a damn how it looks. I want to be there for my daughter.''

The bell rang again. Anxiously Ava glanced at the door.

"You don't have to spend the night, you can go back to Rita's, but I think it's important for Lily to have both of us around.'' Jared took that opportunity to lean in and whisper in her ear, "If you're worried about me laying a hand on you again, don't.''

She shivered from head to toe, her nipples tightening inside her cotton bra. It was his breath fanning her ear and that spicy scent that was only him causing her to react like this. Her body remembered him so well and craved more. She *was* worried, as he'd said. She was worried that if he didn't touch her she'd go out of her mind with want.

But more than anything, she was worried about

breaking her heart further when he rejected the sexual advances she was more than likely to lob his way.

"I'm not looking to rewrite history," he said, then eased back from her sensitive earlobe.

"Neither am I," she said, the bold-faced lie almost too obvious to be believed. "I just didn't want you to get sick, too, with all the work you must have to—"

"I don't care if I come down with measles or chicken pox," he assured her. "I want to be with my daughter." He crossed his arms over his chest. "Don't tell me that you're willing to go against the doctor's orders because you don't want to be around me."

"Of course not. I will always do what's best for my child."

"And so will I."

Ava released a breath, trying to mentally calm her body and mind at the same time. What was she supposed to do? She really didn't want move Lily. And Jared deserved to care for his child, didn't he? It was just for a few days. She could handle being around him without exploding for a few days.

Couldn't she?

"Fine," she said at last. "We'll stay until Lily's better."

"Good. Now go let your sister in and I'll finish up with the doctor."

After he walked back into he living room, Ava ambled to the door at a snail's pace and opened it with about as much enthusiasm.

"It's about time." Rita stood on the front porch with two suitcases, her blue eyes flashing. "What were you doing in there?"

"Oh, please." Ava shouldered her way out the door and closed it behind her, then took a seat on the steps.

A brilliant blue sky decorated the heavens and a light breeze blew the fresh morning scents of earth and sunshine about her face. But even the perfect day couldn't soothe her.

Rita plunked down beside her. "How's my niece?"

"Her fever's down and she's sleeping. The doctor said it's just a little bug. Nothing to worry about."

"I'm glad." She poked Ava in the arm with her elbow. "And how's my sister?"

"You can wipe that smile off your face. Seriously. This is no laughing matter. Jared has insisted we stay here until Lily's better."

"So I gathered. Imagine my surprise while in the middle of my morning yoga I received a phone call from my sister's—"

"Don't even say it," Ava warned, narrowing her eyes.

Rita put her hands up in surrender. "All right. I won't say another word. I won't say that you look somehow different today. And I surely won't say that your eyes are glowing just like they did way back when you first saw Daddy's new ranch hand."

"Don't you have a handsome sheikh to marry?" Ava muttered.

"Not for a few more days."

Ava watched Rita's expression turn from playful to thoughtful, and she put a hand on hers. "What's wrong?"

"Nothing." Rita shook her head, gave Ava a wide smile that didn't reach her eyes. "Hey, I don't want to be the only married Thompson. Get it in gear and make Jared realize that he's never fallen out of love with you."

Ava's heart plunged to her stomach.

"Just remember," Rita continued. "Reminiscing can lead to all sorts of fun situations."

Yeah, it sure could, Ava mused. In fact after their little Milky Way discussion last night she'd hardly slept a wink. And when she *had* closed her eyes, all she saw was them together, legs intertwined, lips parted, hands exploring.

Rita fiddled with the luggage tag on Ava's bag. "You know, you should be happy that he's so interested in his child, Ava—that he's already head over heels for her."

"I am. Of course, I am. It's not his affection for Lily that I'm worried about."

"It's his affection for you?"

"No."

"It's your affection for him?"

Ava glared at her. "If you still want me to be your maid of honor, you'd better can it."

"Speaking of which," Rita said, standing up and brushing a little dirt from her jean-clad backside. "Don't forget about my better-late-than-never engagement lunch Friday afternoon."

"If Lily's feeling up to it, you know I'll definitely be there."

Rita winked at her. "You can even bring a date," Then she waved and loped down the steps.

Ava groaned, stood up, picked up the luggage and headed into the house, calling, "Bye, Rita," over her shoulder.

Jared couldn't help himself.

They looked like a little slice of heaven to him.

He stood in the doorway of Lily's room and watched Ava try to coax the little girl into eating. Ava spoke softly, sweetly, with loving words. It made his heart ache with longing to join them. But as she'd given him time alone with Lily this afternoon he felt she deserved the same courtesy.

He smiled as he thought about his time with Lily earlier. He'd read to her until she'd fallen asleep, then sat in a chair and watched her, wondering what she had looked like as a baby. Had her breathing changed since then? Had her hands always curled around the pillow like that? Had they always looked like his mother's hands?

Lily glanced up then and spied him. "Hi, Jared."

Ava looked over her shoulder and smiled a little shyly. No doubt she was wondering how long he'd been standing there.

"What smells so good?" he asked, wandering into the room.

"Mommy made me chicken soup with rice in it."

"Mmm," he said, sitting down on the opposite side of the bed from Ava. "I love chicken soup. It's my favorite."

Lily's face brightened. "Me, too."

"Then why aren't you eating?"

Ava looked at him. "She thinks it will make her tummy hurt again."

Jared let loose a soft, "Ahh," of understanding, then glanced back to his daughter. She was such a precious sight. Her long, copper hair falling about her flushed face, cuddled up in pajamas with little paw prints all over it. "My grandfather used to say that when a child got sick it was their time to rebuild their spirit. To make them strong in mind and in body for an important journey."

Lily's eyes widened. "What's my journey, Jared?"

He shrugged. "It could be helping me with Tayka when she has her foal. But we don't want to risk that—not unless you're strong."

The little girl gasped, then turned to Ava. "I want my soup, Mommy."

Ava glanced over at Jared, a mother's approval in her eyes. He winked at her, feeling as though he'd just won a million dollars, as though he'd taken the first step into the mysterious world of parenting.

Lily ate half the bowl of soup before she looked up at Ava with droopy eyes. "I'm tired, Mommy."

"Okay, baby. You rest now."

Lily's eyes closed and she was on her way to dream land in moments as Jared whispered a good-night to her and picked up the tray.

Ava gave her little girl a kiss on her forehead. "Temperature's down," she whispered to Jared as she walked to the door and switched off the light.

"Good. Remember to keep the door open a crack," he said in the hallway. "She likes that."

Ava smiled softly at him. "Yes, she does."

She walked ahead of him on the stairs and he couldn't help but take in her curves, her long, tanned legs—and the way her hips swayed as she moved down the steps.

He cleared his throat, hoping to clear his mind along with it. He needed to stay away from thoughts like that.

Far away.

"The soup smells great," he said. "I didn't know you could cook."

"Yep. Some people have told me that I'm quite the gourmet."

"Your husband one of them?"

She froze at the bottom of the stairs, said nothing.

He shouldn't be asking, but he couldn't help himself. Now that he knew Lily was his, the need to know about the man who raised her was strong. And he had nothing to go on. The PI he'd hired was still working on finding out everything he could about Ava's ex-husband.

Stiffly Ava walked toward the kitchen. "My friends tell me that I'm a good cook," she said, strain threading her voice. "I used to have theme nights once a month. Italian, Mexican, Indian."

"That sounds like a good time." He followed her and placed the tray on the counter. "So, what line of work did you say your husband's in?"

"I didn't," she said tightly.

"I thought you did. Well, what does he do?"

She poured some soap into the sink and flipped on the water, began to wash the dishes. "Why do you want to know about him?"

"I want to know about the man who was a father figure to my child."

"Lily never had a father figure. We…well, we weren't together that long."

"Fine. Then I want to know about the guy who walked away from a woman and a baby."

"Why are you so sure he left me?"

"Did he leave you, Ava?"

She said nothing, scrubbing the bowl with a little too much vigor.

"Did he leave you when he found out that you were carrying another man's child?" Jared pressed.

"Something like that," she ground out.

"Bastard," Jared hissed. "You should have called me."

"I did call you, Jared." She shut off the water with a snap, then turned to face him, her eyes blazing emerald fire. "You know I did." A flash of soapsuds flew through the air and hit Jared square on the jaw.

He touched his face and came back with a handful of pink suds. Ava's gaze rested on the cloud of pink and she bit her lip, her eyes turning from angry to surprised to animated.

Jared's eyes narrowed. "You want me off this subject pretty bad, don't you?"

"I do, but I didn't mean to take it to the water fight level." She covered her mouth, but couldn't suppress what was coming. She burst out laughing. "I'm sorry."

He grinned in spite of himself and leaned past her, dipping into the sink. "Oh, not nearly as sorry as you're gonna be."

Ava's eyes widened with mock alarm. "Do we really want to go down this road?"

"You started it."

"It's pretty immature, don't you think?"

"Nope." He scooped up a handful of suds.

"What would you call it then?" she asked, half laughing as she reached behind her back and scooped up her own handful of suds.

He took a step forward, standing within inches of her, his target. "Taking my revenge."

Before she could say a word, he'd smeared the watery suds down her blouse. She froze, then gasped, then glanced down at her wet top.

He leaned forward, his hands falling against the counter on either side of her. "You were saying?"

Her eyes alight with play, she uttered, "You're going down, Redwolf."

She moved quickly. Tossing her handful of suds right at his face. Jared ducked and shot back away from her. Quick as lightning, Ava moved to the sink for more. But Jared was right beside her. For a good five minutes, they pummeled each other with water and suds, laughing hysterically until both of their shirts were soaked through.

"Had enough, Thompson?"

"Not a chance, Redwolf."

But just as Ava reached for another handful of suds, Jared snaked an arm around her waist, grabbed both of her wrists with one hand and held her against him. Bubbles floated in the air around them.

"You're all wet," she said breathlessly.

He chuckled. "So are you."

The smile died on his lips as he slowly became aware of how close she was, and how transparent her shirt was. If he moved away from her just an inch he could see for himself. Dammit, he felt her—the fullness of her breasts, her nipples tightening beneath her wet clothes. She felt altogether new in his arms, yet familiar. And the combination stirred his blood like a Cheyenne Sun Dance.

Without another thought, he lowered his mouth and kissed her. Nearly sighed. Her lips were so warm, so soft. Just as he remembered. And she was so willing.

Jared tried like hell to keep from touching her but it was no use. She arched toward him as she returned his kiss, her lips parting, her tongue darting out.

It was lunacy to walk away from such an invitation now.

No, it was impossible.

Holding her wrists in one hand, as he knew if she touched him his mind would dissolve into a puddle on the cool kitchen tiles, he eased the other under her wet shirt and up her torso. She made a soft moaning sound against his mouth—the sound that had always driven him crazy with need—and he cupped her breast through the thin fabric of her bra.

They stood there, her back against the sink, his thigh between her legs, his fingers coaxing her nipple into pebble hardness as they made out like two ravenous teenagers.

Until the phone rang.

Then again.

And once more.

"Don't you have to get that?" Ava asked, pulling back just slightly, her eyes blazing with emerald heat, her mouth pink and wet from his kiss.

"The machine'll pick it up."

Through a red haze of desire, he heard his own voice on the tape, short and clipped. "You've reached Redwolf Industries. Please leave a message. Thank you." Then he heard a woman's voice. Irritated, but seductive. He froze, his lips hovering just above Ava's, his erection pressing into her belly. "Jared, honey. Where are you? I've been waiting, sitting here in that tight, black—"

Releasing Ava, Jared cursed and dove for the machine, hitting the mute button with ferocity. Wednesday. It was Wednesday. The night he spent with Tina.

He turned to face Ava and hated what he saw.

She was hugging her arms to her chest, her mouth tight and grim. "Looks like you have plans."

He exhaled heavily. "With Lily getting sick, I completely forgot."

"You don't need to explain."

"I didn't think—"

"It's none of my business." Her gaze swept the floor, then returned to him. She looked somber with a tone of voice to match. ''I'll let you clean up this mess. Good night.''

She turned and walked out of the room and Jared fought the urge to call her back or run after her, haul her into his arms again. She'd felt like heaven, like he remembered and he wanted more. He wanted to make love to her, here on this floor—the way he'd imagined a thousand times. But he couldn't. Sure, his anger and resentment were subsiding, but there was a more practical reason for him to keep his distance.

Ava didn't belong to him.

Never had and never would.

He should've been with Tina, he told himself sternly, grabbing a roll of paper towels and spreading the sheets out over the wet floor. Uncomplicated and unfulfilling, but always reliable. He had come to appreciate those qualities in a sexual encounter.

But he didn't want Tina. He didn't want to be with any other woman. Not now. Not after *she'd* come back into his life. Not after he'd touched her again, smelled her skin.

No, he wanted Ava. Under him, moaning his name.

Beneath his feet, the towels soaked up the water, seeping slowly across the paper, inch by inch, just like his resolve.

He raked a hand through his hair. Nothing had changed. Not his desire for her in his bed or in his heart. But there was one thing he knew for sure. He was going to fight like hell to keep her out of both.

Seven

Ava pushed her empty cart up and down the canned food aisle of the Killer Chicken Market for the third time that afternoon.

Why had she come back here?

The question nagged at her. Why had she come here? Not to the market, but to Paradise. It wasn't just for Rita's wedding. She'd known that the minute she'd stepped off the plane a week ago. Her sister's wedding had been the excuse she'd been waiting for, certainly, but not the purpose.

No, she'd come back to face Jared. Finally tell him the truth. And she'd come to see if he had any residual feelings left for her or if her quick departure out of town four years ago had quashed all sentiment in his heart.

But after the night before last she still had no clear-cut answers.

Over the last several days, she and Jared had gone about their lives without intimate discussion. During the day, he hung out with Lily, playing games and reading to her. At night, Ava would cuddle with her and sing her to sleep. Then later, when the house was quiet, she and Jared would casually end up in the living room, talk for a bit then make their way upstairs to separate bedrooms.

Clearly that encounter in the kitchen was weighing heavily on both their minds, she thought, recalling how Jared's eyes would fill with longing whenever he looked her way.

She could only imagine that her own gaze mirrored his.

"My husband and I are looking into buying the Thompson place when it goes up for sale."

The feminine and plainly older high-pitched chatter in the next aisle caught Ava's attention immediately and she scooted closer to the pickled beets to listen.

"Ben Thompson is selling his land?" the second woman asked. "He's had that ranch for too many years to count."

"It's the rumor about town, Sara, that's all I'm saying. He just can't keep up the place now."

"What a pity."

"Not for Carl and I."

"Sheri-Ann, that's terrible!" Sara scolded.

Sheri-Ann lowered her voice a fraction, which wasn't saying much. "Serves the man right, I say. He treated his workers pretty poorly and his daughters worse."

Ava felt a rumble of sadness in her chest. Yes, her father hadn't been kind to his workers and had treated her abominably. The women weren't wrong about that.

But he *was* her father after all, and there was nothing that straightened a person's spine and lifted her nose more than someone insulting the only family a person had—truth or not.

"Some say he's a changed man since that car sideswiped him a few years back," Sara said.

"Don't know anything about that. But I ask you, how much can a man his age really change?"

The women continued in opposition down the aisle, their voices growing slightly muffled as they went. Ava glanced to her right, her stomach tightening. Soon they'd be coming up her aisle. Soon they'd see her and realize who she was and what she'd heard them say. There was a part of her that wanted to see their faces when that happened. But the other part just wanted to get the heck out of Dodge before everyone got embarrassed as they tried to explain away their callous commentary.

So she rolled her cart in the opposite direction and headed for the produce section for salad fixings. But as hard as she tried to shut it out, her mind remained focused on the overheard conversation. For as much as she wanted to agree with Sheri-Ann's take on her father's lack of change, she couldn't help but wonder if he really had. And if he had, would she ever be able to give him a chance to prove it?

"Are you sure?"

"I'm at the hall of records right now, Mr. Redwolf."

As the last rays of the day's sun filtered through the window behind him, Jared sat forward at his desk, gripping the phone so tightly he wouldn't have been surprised if it had broken in half. "They could've been married out of state."

"Nope," the private detective said. "My buddy at the FBI did some checking on that. Never happened."

"What about Lily's birth certificate?"

"No father listed. Just the mother. I'm telling you, this lady was never married."

Muttering an oath, Jared dropped back in his chair and swiveled away from his desk and around to face the floor-to-ceiling windows that provided a crystal-clear view of his substantial acreage.

"Why the hell would she tell me…?"

Jared didn't finish the question as the detective grunted and said, "You might find this interesting."

"What's that?"

"In all the time Miss Thompson lived in New York, she never dated."

"Say that again."

Jared could hear the detective flipping through pages. "At least we couldn't come up with a name. And you know how thorough we are."

Yes. Jared did know. After thanking the man, he hung up the phone and rubbed a hand over his jaw. He didn't have a clue how to feel about this news. In one sense he was glad that no other man had a claim on Lily, that no other man had touched her mother. He also felt shocked that Ava hadn't dated in four years. But the strongest emotion that stirred in his blood was anger.

Ava had lied to him about the husband.

She'd lied to him again.

For one brief second he wondered if she'd lied to him about Lily being his child. But the thought was gone in an instant. He could see himself and Muna and his mother in Lily. And more important, he could feel, just as Muna had, that the little girl was his.

So why then? Why had Ava gone to New York if it wasn't for another man? And why lie about it? Was it as he'd suspected? When she'd found out she was pregnant, had she felt that Jared couldn't support them? Or was there more? More she wasn't telling him?

Jared jerked to his feet, walked to the window, stared into the heart of the ginger sunset. How had things gotten so tricky? He was angry with the woman who had given him Lily. He was angry with the woman he desired more than anything in the world. He was angry with the woman who made him so happy and carefree when she was near.

Where had his resolve escaped to when he needed it most?

His hands balled into fists at his side. He wanted to confront Ava about what he'd learned. Yet, he didn't want to hear the answer. All he wanted—all he'd wanted from the moment he'd seen her in Benton's Bridal and Formalwear—was her in his arms, her whispering in his ear as he pushed into her body.

Just once more.

To remember, and to forget.

Just once more to get her out of his mind and his soul.

Muttering an oath, he stalked to the door and headed out to find his sanity in the only place it dwelled.

Overhead, the full moon gleamed opal, lighting a pathway up the curve of hill. Beside Ava, Tim Donahue, Jared's brawny ranch foreman, guided the trek while all around them, the wild, yelping call of prowling cougars, though far off, seemed to encircle the twosome as they walked the Redwolf land.

But being in the midst of this wild territory was only

part of the reason Ava's heart thudded nervously in her chest. Several yards away, a fire smoldered in a deep pit, while behind it sat Jared's sweat lodge, a brown dome-like structure supported by several wood poles. She'd heard Jared speak of such a place way back when they'd shared such intimacies, but she'd never seen him create one.

Odds were, he hadn't been too keen on building a sweat lodge on her father's land. Nor would her father have permitted it.

"Here we are, ma'am."

Ava glanced up at the handsome older man and smiled. "Thanks, Tim."

"He's not going to be happy you've come. Not right away anyway. Give him some time."

"I don't have much time."

He grinned. "You know something, Miss Thompson?"

"Ava, please."

HIs grin widened. "He wants to forgive you."

It took Ava a moment to register what he'd just said, a little stunned by the directness of it all. "Does he?"

Tim nodded. "Just doesn't know how. Afraid to, I expect. But you'll help him won't you, Ava?"

Tim didn't wait for an answer, merely grasped the brim of his Stetson, gave her a quick wink and walked off down the path and over the hill.

Ava stared after him for a moment, thinking about what he'd said, wondering if it was true—if it were possible. Then she turned back to the sweat lodge and pressed onward.

Feeling as though she was trespassing on sacred ground, she trod lightly as she walked past the fire pit and up to the tarp door of the lodge. The scent of smoke was intense and she could hear a deep, rhythmic and incredibly beautiful sound coming from inside.

It was Jared, chanting, praying.

But for what, she could only wonder.

Her hand paused against the warm green tarp, wondering for a moment if it would be best if she turned around, ran to find Tim, headed back to the house. After all, she could speak to him about such practical matters later. But something out of her realm of understanding forced her hand, then guided her through the door.

A blast of intense heat assaulted her body while the scent of smoke and sage shot into her nostrils, making them burn. Swallowing the grit in her throat, she rubbed a hand over her eyes to clear her vision. It was dark inside the sweat lodge; just the light from several smooth melon-size stones in a smoldering pit in front of her illuminated the room.

Damp with sweat, she squinted as her eyes became accustomed to the dimness. Then she saw him. Sitting nude before the pit, his head down, his black hair falling past his shoulders.

"Jared?"

He looked up slowly, his face wet with sweat, his eyes glowing with a passion she couldn't name.

Her heart jolted with awareness.

"You seem to continually find me naked," he said, his voice lazy, husky.

"It's not by design, I promise you."

"Are you sure?"

She made the mistake of hesitating a second too long, and a dark grin tugged at his full mouth.

"Well, this time I refuse to cover up," he said. "You're in my space, my sanctuary."

"True," she said, the intensity of the heat baking her skin, the intensity of his gaze imprisoning her heart.

"And besides, you've seen it all before, isn't that right?" he said as he poured water onto the rocks, making them glow and hiss.

"Well—"

"I meant the male form, Ava. Your husband certainly…"

"Right. My husband." She shifted from one foot to the other.

"Did he look like me?"

"What? What do you mean?"

Jared stood, his nude, wet skin glistening in the dim light. "Was he smooth like me or did he have hair?"

Ava swallowed hard. "I don't—"

"Remember?"

She made no move to answer him. How could she? How could she with him standing there, staring at her like he was? So beautiful. So tall, long, lean, all sharp angles, so proud as the sublime maleness of him grew hard beneath her gaze. And though she could barely breathe from the smothering heat inside the tent, her legs itched to run toward him, her fingers itched to touch him, run her palms up his smooth, finely muscled chest to his neck, then deep into his hair, and finally to the back of his head, pulling him down to her mouth.

"We were talking about your husband," he said tightly, crossing his arms over his chest.

Her heart sank. "I know."

"Was he tall like me?"

"No."

"Did his eyes move over every inch of your skin the way mine did?"

"Jared—"

He wasn't about to give up. "Did he feel like me, Ava? Did he feel like me when he was inside you?"

She colored fiercely, her legs feeling disturbingly water-filled as her gaze flickered down his body once more. "Maybe I... I can meet you back at the house to talk—"

"You're uncomfortable."

"The heat's oppressive."

"It must be to cleanse the soul, to ask for what we desire most—and desire to be rid of." He brushed off a bead of sweat winding its way down his neck. "But I know what will make you feel more at ease."

"Do you?"

He nodded. "Take off your clothes."

"What?" She fairly choked out the word.

"Take off your clothes, sit beside me—or under me—" his eyes darkened dangerously "—and we'll... talk."

Ava waited for the slam of shock she expected to ripple through her body, but it never came. She'd come here to talk, yes, about Lily, about life after Rita's wedding, but if truth be told she'd also come here to be with him, around him and even beneath him if he was really serious in his offer. The truth was, when he wasn't near, when she couldn't hear his voice, she felt completely disconnected. Jared Redwolf had been such an enormous part of her life, both as a flesh and blood man and as a fantasy that she'd grown accustomed— no, addicted—to loving him.

"Mulling it over?" he asked with a slight edge to his voice.

"Just weighing the pros and cons."

He chuckled enigmatically. "You should know that

with me the pros far outweigh the cons." His lips tightened. "But perhaps you don't remember—"

"I remember." Ava said the words with such vehemence that they actually elicited a smile, a genuine smile, from Jared.

His gaze swept her. "I could direct you."

"What do you mean?"

"With your clothing. I could direct you." He raised a brow at her. "First you must remove your socks and shoes. They have no place here."

She bit her lip, tasted her own sweat. If she started this, where would it end? If they made love, where would it end?

No answers came and she didn't fight herself for them. She was ready to be touched by this man again. It was her destiny, her right. She bent down and took off her socks and shoes.

"Now your jacket," he commanded softly.

Her gaze found his and with trembling hands, she did as he commanded.

"Your shirt must go next."

Slowly she unbuttoned her white blouse, shrugged out of it and let it fall to the dirt floor below.

Jared's gaze dipped, taking in the bra she wore, the pale pink silk damp with sweat. A muscle flicked in his jaw and he muttered, "Jeans."

Her fingers reached for button and zipper as she kept her gaze locked with his. With her heart pounding in her ears, she slipped out of her pants, feeling no cooler as she tossed them aside.

His gaze fierce with hunger, Jared walked around the pit and stood before her. "I'll help you with these last two."

She held her arms out to her sides. Her defenses

were completely gone now, given in to the man before her, the man she'd loved for so long. She nodded in surrender. With a slow grin, Jared reached up and unhooked her bra in one easy motion. Ava couldn't help but smile in return. He'd done the same on their first night together and she'd never forgotten it.

But her smile quickly faded when Jared eased off the silky fabric altogether and she stood before him nude from the waist up.

Heat suffused her breasts, tickled her nipples, the rosy peaks beading with desire as Jared palmed her stomach, then pressed downward, down to the edge of her panties. Ava sucked in a breath, waiting, wondering if he would feel as amazing as she remembered.

But Jared didn't slide the slip of silk over her hips. Instead he eased a hand down, inside the damp fabric.

Ava released the breath she was holding, let her eyes drift closed, let her mind shut off.

His mouth inches from hers, his breath scented with sage, he whispered, "You're so warm."

"It's you," she uttered hoarsely.

He didn't respond to her compliment, said instead, "What did you come here to say, Ava?"

Eyes still shut, she shook her head. "I don't remember."

His fingers drifted lower, played in her woman's hair for just a moment before settling into the wet lips beneath. "You sure you don't remember?" he asked.

She could only nod, not entirely sure if asked if she recall her own name.

"Was it about your life?" he asked, his fingers drifting back and forth over the bundle of nerves at her core.

She arched her back, then thrust her hips toward him,

silently pleading with him to put her out of her misery, to thrust his fingers inside of her. Never in her life had she wanted something so much as Jared inside her in any way possible.

He nuzzled her neck, but didn't kiss her as he whispered against her skin, "Was it about your husband?"

"What?" She heard the question in her head and cursed into the hot air around them. "No!"

He lifted his head, his mouth now hovering above hers. "You know I'm not going to give up on this subject."

"Jared, please—" she begged.

"Tell me about your husband."

"There was no husband, all right?" she practically shouted.

"No?"

"No!" Ava opened her eyes, stared up at him, her body so consumed with need she was almost to the point of pain. "There's never been anyone but you."

After searching her gaze for one brief moment, Jared nodded, "That's what I wanted to hear," then thrust his fingers deep inside her.

Ava gasped, needing air, needing more. She pumped her hips, taking him in and out of her body as she forced her mind to close. She wouldn't admonish herself for blurting out the truth. No, she was glad it was done. She wouldn't ask herself why he didn't seem surprised at her admission, either. She wouldn't ask because at that moment she didn't care. All she wanted was Jared's touch. It had been too long since a man had touched her—and this man was all she'd ever wanted.

Jared worked her like a man who knew her inside and out, a man who knew how to make her scream

with desire. But he didn't kiss her, didn't speak, didn't
even moan as he played her body. He just held her
against him, thrusting his fingers deeper and deeper
inside her.

Flashes of pure pleasure, of the orgasm to come,
rippled through Ava and she smiled to herself. How
could a woman want to climax yet not want to climax
all in the same moment? Well, she had little choice in
the matter as Jared began to flick the sensitive skin
beneath her slick, wet folds.

She tried to hold on, but it was no use. Electricity
shuddered through her, pounded her senses. The feeling
was relentless and she shattered completely. Breathing
heavily and whimpering her last waves of pleasure, she
sagged against him.

But only for a moment.

She didn't want to rest. She wanted her body wet
and sensitized and tight when he eased himself over
her, entered her with one single hard thrust.

"Jared," she uttered as she slid her hand down his
groin and fisted the steely length of him.

"No." He backed away, dropping his hands from
her, leaving her desperate.

Her breathing still slightly ragged, she stared at him,
sweat dripping down her neck and into her cleavage.
"Why are you stopping?"

His eyes were cold, passionless. "I gave you what
you needed."

Her pulse stumbled. "What about what you need?"

He shook his head, then walked past her, lifted the
tarp door and flipped it over the top of the lodge. "Not
here. Not now."

She didn't understand what was happening, why he

was suddenly acting cold as ice. "We can go back to the house—"

"No. I won't take pleasure from you."

"What?"

"I don't trust you, Ava." He didn't cover himself as he walked out the door, calling back, "And I'm not sure if I ever will."

Sweaty and drained of all rational thought and understanding, Ava stood at the entrance to the lodge and watched him walk away, into the night, beautiful, naked and cruel.

Eight

Jared found Muna in her workroom, dying the plant materials she'd gathered in the canyons and creek bottoms close to Redwolf Ranch. For a moment, he just watched her work the reeds into the deep, rich red pigment for she was truly a site to see. A timeless site. Long salt-and-pepper braids hung forward as she spoke lovingly to the plants, asking them to grant her the right to weave them into one of her plaited baskets.

No doubt sensing his presence, Muna stilled over her work, but didn't turn around. "Where are they?" she asked softly.

Accustomed to her extraordinary sensitivities, Jared didn't even cut a smile, but walked into the room and dropped down into a chair beside the dye bath. "They went to Ben's place for lunch. Something about Rita's wedding."

Muna nodded. "Ava took Little Star with her?"

"Yes."

"She is well enough?"

"Ava thought so."

Looking up, Muna studied her grandson. "You wish she had invited you?"

"What?" He fairly choked over the words. "No!"

"What is this anger I feel from your spirit?"

Jared scrubbed a hand over his face. His grand-mother's sensitivities could be extremely helpful at times, but today her abilities filled him with nothing but frustration.

Ava had left an hour ago for her father's ranch and had taken Lily with her. After they'd driven off, Jared had instantly headed to his office, ready to tackle the pile of work that was stacked up on his desk. But trying to work in his state of mind had proven futile. And he'd escaped to the stables, then to Muna.

Jared wasn't ready to admit it, even to himself, but Muna was right on track. He *was* angry—angry that Ava hadn't asked him to go with them, angry that he missed not just his daughter, but Ava as well.

Ava.

Would she forever haunt him?

After last night, he should've expected his guts to be tied up in knots. Tossing and turning in his bed, his body tight with need, tangled in sheets he'd wished were her long, smooth legs.

"She is growing up."

Jared jerked back to reality, and acknowledged Muna's comment with a nod. "I know. I can't believe my daughter's—"

"No, not Lily," Muna corrected gently. "Ava."

"Ava?"

"She is coming into her own."

"What do you mean?"

Muna placed a willow strand in water, let it sit for a moment to soften. "She has chosen forgiveness over resentment, over anger." She gave him a telling stare. "I think to hold on to such destructive emotions is childlike."

Jared's lips thinned with irritation. "As I have done, you mean?"

"It is not my place to say, but—"

"But you will anyway. Yes, I know."

"Jared, you have done well for yourself. For both of us. Why tighten your hold on this bitterness for Ava and her father?"

Teeth clenched, Jared ground out, "Ben Thompson deserves all of my anger and more."

"But to what end? What is it you seek to gain?"

The room felt suddenly oppressive, its pale orange walls closing in around Jared. "I want the man who made us suffer to suffer himself."

Muna shook her head sadly. "I have never suffered at the hand of Ben Thompson."

"How can you say that?" Jared snorted with derision and kicked a reed of willow with his boot. "We lived in a two-room shack on that man's land before he kicked us out onto the street."

Chin lifted proudly, Muna said, "Again I say that I have never suffered."

"What would you call it then?"

"One ripple, one stone on a beautiful river."

"More like a jagged rock, ready to rip into the flesh if not careful."

"I did not raise you to see life's journey this way."

Jared jerked to his feet. "Perhaps it's my father's legacy to me, then."

Pity and sadness tattooed Muna's face. "I love you, Jared. Tread carefully over the ground you are sowing."

His chest tight with irritation, Jared stood there for a moment, watching as Muna returned to her work, her warning an end to their conversation.

His grandmother was wise, but too kind, too forgiving. Regardless of her unwelcome caveat, Ben Thompson would pay for what he'd done. To Muna and himself, certainly, but to Ava and Lily as well.

Storming out of the room, he went directly to his office. After falling into his chair, he grabbed the phone and punched in the number to his attorney. He was going to make sure when Thompson's ranch went on the market, he would be its first and highest bidder.

She hadn't been back in four years.

With a lump in her throat, Ava glanced around her old bedroom. Nothing had changed. The same butter-yellow paint coated the walls. Same four-poster maple bed sat invitingly in the center of the room, dressed up in that green, yellow and white comforter she'd had since she was twelve. Same lamps and writing desk. Same scent of dried flowers and pencil erasers from her many nights of journaling.

And the same bookcase with the pale green hearts she'd painted on it in tenth grade.

Ava smiled as she recalled what was written on the exposed wood backing of that bookcase.

Ava loves Jared.

And in caps— *FOREVER*.

Her smile faded a touch. After last night's humiliation, she should feel anything but sentimentality toward Jared Redwolf. At first he'd treated her with tenderness and mind-numbing heat, then cut her flat. He'd made it clear he had no interest in her anymore—that he felt only contempt wrapped in a bubble of lust.

Grief swam heavily in her blood and she felt tears prick her eyes. Once upon a time, he had loved her so...

"Nice posters of Van Halen, sis," Rita said, coming up beside her.

Rita. That's what she needed to concentrate on. Her sister and her upcoming marriage, and the wonder of such a beautiful person getting all she deserved.

"Seriously," Rita continued, elbowing Ava in the ribs. "I can't believe you kept those up until you were twenty."

"I can't believe Dad has kept them up since," Ava said on a laugh.

"Yeah, well, just goes to show how much he missed you."

"Right."

"It's true, big sister."

Ava switched gears and went to sit on the bed—the lumpy mattress dipping low as it always had. "Lily still on the tour of the ranch?"

Rita followed suit and sat next to her sister. "Yep. Hand in hand with her grandpa."

Hand in hand. Ava mentally shook her head. Her father had never held her hand. Not once. Forcing down the twinge of envy she felt, she said, "I've never seen her so happy."

Rita grinned. "Getting a father and a grandfather all in one week could do that to a child."

"Especially a child like her."

"She's wanted them for a long time, huh? Or the promise of them?"

Ava sighed. "You have no idea."

"I'm glad Sakir and I decided to get married, then." Rita winked. "Got you and Lil out here."

"Well, the promise of seeing her auntie Rita was a major selling point, I have to say."

Fluffing her hair in a show of flash, Rita said, "What a lucky kid."

Ava laughed. It was so great hanging out with her sister again. "By the way, where is this mysterious sheikh of yours?"

Rita's blue eyes clouded a touch. "He got called out of town. But he sends his regards."

"Regards, huh…pretty fancy."

"Yeah, he's something else all right."

"No groom at his own wedding lunch," Ava said, fingering the faded quilt her mother had made when she was five. "So, what? I'm not going to meet this guy until the day of your wedding?"

Coming to her feet, Rita walked over to the window and stared out. "That could very well happen."

"You love him, don't you Rita?"

"Of course."

The disquiet in Rita's tone worried Ava. She didn't like that she hadn't met the man her sister was about to marry. She felt it was her job as older sister, not to mention maid of honor, to grill the man, make sure he was worthy of her sister.

"We'd better go downstairs," Rita said, turning

around, tugging Ava from her thoughts and giving her a bright smile. "We could offer Maria a hand while we ply her with questions about her romance with Dad."

"I still don't get that."

"What? How dad was a huge bigot and is now dating a stunning Mexican woman?"

"Yeah, that."

Laughing, Rita walked over to Ava and held out her hand. "Ever heard of the saying, 'people can change'?"

Ava placed her hand in Rita's and let her sister pull her up. "Once or twice, but I never would've imagined it applied to him."

"Me, neither, but he has, and you need to forgive him. Give him a chance to explain and apologize."

Ava followed her sister out the door and down the hall, tension building inside her at her sister's comments. If the man really had changed, why couldn't he have done it earlier? When Jared was a part of her life and he loved her and could've been a father to Lily— maybe even a husband to her?

Husband…

The word stuck in her mind and pecked at her heart. She'd forgotten about what Jared had said last night— what she'd said to him about having no husband. Why, she wondered now, hadn't he seemed surprised when she'd blurted out the truth?

As she walked down the stairs she made a silent vow to ask him about his lack of reaction when she and Lily returned to the ranch tonight.

"Just like old times, girls."

At the bottom of the steps stood her father, dressed

casually in jeans and a clean work shirt. He was smiling, his wrinkled, tanned hand outstretched in welcome. Ava stiffened. She couldn't help it.

Rita grabbed her hand and squeezed.

"Hi, Dad," Ava said tentatively. "Thanks for having us over for lunch."

The man's eyes were gentle as his smile broadened. "Thank you for coming, Ava. And for bringing my granddaughter."

"We saw Auntie Rita and grandpa and the ranch and all the animals," Lily said, then dropped back against the bed pillows and yawned.

Jared covered his daughter up to her chin with the pale gray comforter, then tucked the sides up under her good and tight like she liked it. He was getting too used to this wonderful routine. Reading to her, tucking her in, their hushed conversations as she slowly drifted off sleep.

"Did you see the big tree right outside the kitchen door?" he asked her, not adding that it was the place where he and Ava had shared their first kiss.

"Yeah. I bet it'll grow up to heaven, don't you think?"

"Easily."

Lily smiled broadly. "And guess what?"

"What?"

"I saw Maria, too?"

"Maria? Who's Maria, Little Star?"

"Grandpa's girlfriend."

Jared hesitated, not sure if he'd heard her correctly. "Your grandpa has a girlfriend?"

Lily nodded slowly. "She's from Mexico, and she's pretty and cooks yummy stuff with corn and cheese."

Baffled and sort of unnerved, Jared sat back in his chair. Ben was dating a Mexican woman? One of the foremost bigots in Paradise? Impossible. Lily had to be wrong.

"Time for your reading, Little Star."

It was Muna, coming to sit with Lily as she'd promised, and Jared could only rise from his seat and bite his tongue on the questions he had for his daughter.

Taking Jared's chair, Muna smiled at Lily. "My Little Star will have her future read tonight before her dreams come. You do not mind, do you, Jared?"

"No. 'Course not." He bent and kissed his daughter on the forehead. "Good night, sweetheart."

She grinned at him. "'Night, Jared."

As he walked down the hall toward the stairs, Jared could still hear Muna's rich voice. "Tell me again of the month you were born, Little Star, and we will talk of your future…"

Jared decided against going downstairs for a bite to eat and instead headed to his room. Once there, he made his way to the balcony. He wanted air—which always made him feel better, stronger, as though he could see and hear and think with better clarity under the open sky.

Obviously Ava had the same idea, he mused, stepping out onto the smooth tiled balcony. She was leaning against the waist-high wall, staring out into the starless, earth-scented night. Wearing a white silk tank and matching pajama bottoms, her long blond hair falling loose about her shoulders, she looked like something out of this world. She looked beautiful and he fought the urge to jump the short barrier between them and take her in his arms.

"Can't sleep?"

She stole in a breath, whirled to face him, her hand to her chest. "You startled me."

"I'm sorry."

With a little laugh, she said, "It's fine. Is Lily all right? Did she fuss about going to sleep?"

He shook his head. "Muna's with her. Seems they have a future to discuss before Lily's allowed to sleep."

Leaning back against the balcony, she smiled. "I forgot about that."

"But I'm thinking she'll be asleep within minutes. She looked pretty tired."

"She had a big day."

"So I heard."

The summer night played cool, sending breaths of air back and forth over the plains, back and forth over her skin.

"Listen, Ava I appreciate you letting her stay here even though we both know her flu is long gone."

She shrugged. "You deserve the time with her."

"You mean before you return to New York?" he asked tightly.

"Yes."

"I think leaving Paradise a bad idea."

Her gaze faltered. "My work is there or else I just might consider—"

"Might consider what? Moving back here with your father?"

"Maybe."

"And me?"

Warmth flooded her gaze. "Yes."

Jared didn't know what hit him, but he knew he couldn't be stopped. He leapt easily from his balcony to hers, walked straight for her and took her in his arms possessively. "What else is there to keep you in New York? You have no man. And I know you've never had a husband."

"I... How did you find out—"

"It wasn't hard, Ava."

"But why would you—"

"I wanted to know who might have claims on my daughter."

Her gaze slipped. "Of course."

"My only question is why lie about it?"

She shook her head, turned away.

As the wind picked up around them, Jared slipped a finger under her chin and turned her to face him. "You didn't want me coming after you, did you? You knew if I thought you were with another man, I'd never come after you, isn't that right?"

Tears pricked her eyes. "Yes."

"Damn you, Ava."

Jared bent and took her mouth with fierce determination. He was already hard as hell and ready to make love to her right there against the wall, under the black sky.

"Why did you have to come back here?" he uttered against her mouth.

Swiping his lower lip with her tongue, Ava whispered, "I'm sorry. I'm so sorry."

He couldn't hear her anymore. No words, only the sounds of pleasure were welcome now. Backing away, he cupped her waist and lifted the white tank over her head. She wore no bra, and he stared at her breasts, her nipples dark and swollen.

His body tightened to the point of pain.

Slow and steady lovemaking had no place here, he realized, shedding his own shirt. Not after what they'd experienced in the sweat lodge. Not after the night of sublime frustration he'd barely lived through.

He needed her, needed to consume her and he didn't care what would happen afterward, tomorrow, next week. As he looked into her eyes, he reached for her, filled his hands with her breasts, savoring the weight of them. He knew she'd always loved when he'd touched her there, and she proved it by pressing herself deeper into his palms.

Jared moved to her nipples, and using his thumbs he played them, flicking the very tips until he heard her moan. A deep, cavernous sound that made his chest ache with desire.

No matter how much he wanted to slow his progress, he couldn't wait much longer.

Kneeling down, he eased off her silk pajama bottoms, kissing her exposed skin as he went, the sound of the night animals fueling his quest.

Her belly tasted warm and sweet and he deepened his kiss, lapping at her navel, urging her hips to swing, to dance toward him.

All the while, the scent of her intoxicated him.

No, he could wait no more.

He stood up and Ava reached for him, grabbed his hips, pressed him against her, pressed his jutting arousal against the jointure of her thighs. "No more of this. I want you inside me."

Jared groaned, reached into his back pocket for his

wallet and the condom he knew waited there. He fumbled, but didn't give a damn as she was kissing him, making love to his mouth, telling him what she wanted him to do next with the thrust of her tongue.

He barely got his zipper down before sheathing himself. Barely slid aside the strip of cotton at her waist before entering her.

Ava felt as though she'd died and gone to heaven. She cried out into the night, as though Jared had pierced not only her body but her soul as well. And perhaps he had. He felt so familiar, so perfect in her arms and inside her she wanted to weep.

But he didn't give her the chance.

His head dipped and he took her nipple into his mouth. His thrusts turned wild as he flicked the hard bud back and forth with his tongue.

Ava let her head drop back and gripped the balcony wall for support as the rhythm of his tongue against her swollen nipple quickened. She sucked in a breath, felt the sublime rise of heat building up in her womb.

He tugged and nipped as flesh slapped against flesh.

Flashes of red desire erupted in her belly, then shot lower. She felt him grow harder, thicker and she felt herself stretching to meet his need as he pounded his groin against her tight hips.

She labored for breath, waves of pure pleasure hitting her full on, then rippling. Finally, she gave in, released a guttural moan.

Climax hit full force.

In her ringing ears, she heard Jared take his own pleasure as he drove into her fast and furious.

The moments that followed were hazy. They were filled with slow thrusts and labored breathing. Cool air made its way from the far off plains to their heated skin as Jared nuzzled her neck.

"I always loved the sounds you make," he whispered huskily against her skin.

She smiled. "I hope we didn't wake Lily."

Jared chuckled. "You mean *you* didn't wake Lily."

Easing away from him, she socked him playfully in the arm.

He lifted a brow. "You were the loud one, Thompson, admit it."

"You weren't exactly quiet yourself."

"Don't worry." He leaned in and kissed her mouth gently. "Our daughter is fast asleep."

Our daughter. Did she dare melt right here under the black sky, under the smoky gaze of the man she loved? "She had a wonderful day today."

"Yeah, she told me."

"I hate to say it, but she's so excited to have a grandfather."

Jared's lips thinned and his jaw tightened.

"Please don't look like that," Ava said, warring emotions swelling within her. "I really think that maybe he's changed, Jared."

He stiffened in her arms, then backed up and quickly zipped his fly. "Do we have to talk about your father right now?"

"Why are you so angry with him? If anyone should be angry with him, it's me."

"The man is a fraud, that's why."

She felt very naked suddenly and reached down, grabbed her clothes and pressed them to her breasts. "He may be many things, but he does keep his word."

"What does that mean?"

She plunged on heedlessly. "He took care of you and Muna until you were ready to leave the ranch, didn't he?"

"Your father kicked us off his land a week after you left."

Sheer black rage seeped slowly into her once-heated blood. "What?"

"Just like he didn't want to have to look at his mixed blood granddaughter, he didn't want to have to look at his granddaughter's mixed blood father, either."

Panic—sick, hot panic—rose in Ava's throat. "No, he couldn't have."

"He did."

Ava could barely stand upright. She didn't want to believe what Jared had said, didn't want to think that her father had done such a horrible thing. But in her gut she knew it was true.

And after today…

She sighed, disillusionment enveloping her. She'd had a wonderful conversation with her father after lunch today. He'd apologized for all he'd done and said and had forced her into. But he'd said nothing about this…

Her eyes downcast, she moved away from Jared.

"Where are you going?"

"To check on Lily," she said, slipping her tank back on.

Jared stared at her intently. "Are you coming back?"

She hesitated. What a question. She wanted to, but she felt so tired and unsure and disappointed in herself and her father. She needed to be alone. "I don't think it's wise."

"Right," he said with undisguised bitterness.

The night air seemed suddenly cold and damp. "Jared, for Lily's sake. If she happened to wake up early...seeing us in the morning. She could—" She could develop the same hopes as her mother regarding a future in this house.

"I get it, Ava." Grabbing his shirt, Jared walked away and leaped back over to his balcony. "Have a good night," he called before heading into his room.

And there she was. Again alone. Watching him go.

But this time, she had sent him away.

She fought the tears welling in her throat. Lord, what kind of future, if any, did they have?

Have a good night.

She chuckled with her own bitterness. A good night— She didn't know what that was anymore.

Nine

Jared listened intently as she spoke to her father on the phone. She didn't know he was there and he preferred it that way. At seven this morning he'd heard Ava in the kitchen, making coffee and picking up the phone only to put it back down again a moment later. He'd been on the porch enjoying the sunrise at the time and only when he'd heard her actually start speaking did he scoot his chair closer to the screen door.

He was sure that no matter what Ava asked her father, the man would deny it.

"I need to hear the truth, Dad."

The truth. Jared almost laughed out loud. The man wouldn't know the truth if it rose up and bit him on the—

"I understand that Lily was getting tired and wanted to go home," Ava continued, clearly agitated. "But I would've waited a few minutes. I needed to hear everything you had to say.''

Jared stood up and looked through the window. Brilliant yellow sunlight took up residence in the kitchen, and in contrast, a pale Ava sat on a kitchen stool, grief and confusion in her eyes.

''But why?'' she said, a choked sound to her query. ''Why would you make them leave?''

Jared's thoughts came to a screeching halt. He'd told her. He'd actually told her the truth.

''Do you really expect me to believe that you've changed—that you've suddenly shed this prejudiced cloak you've worn for so long?''

Hearing the sorrow in Ava's voice, the anger inside Jared's heart subsided a touch. He hated himself for softening—hated Ben Thompson for screwing with them all.

He didn't want to hear any more. Her questions or the old man's honesty. In fact, he'd like to get upstairs and drown himself in work. But he couldn't go through the kitchen without Ava seeing him. He'd have to go through the front door.

Halfway down the porch steps, he heard the screen door squeak open.

''Jared?''

Too late. He turned and saw her, eyes a little red, jaw a little tight.

''You were listening?'' she asked.

He nodded, waiting for her certain reproach.

But she didn't scold him for eavesdropping, instead she sat down on the chair that he'd occupied only moments ago and released a weighty sigh. ''I'm sorry.''

''For what?'' he asked tightly.

"For all of this. The lies, the holding back—what my father did to you and Muna. It's—"

"It's over."

"No, it's not. Not between you and me and not between you and him."

Her voice was hoarse with frustration and her eyes implored him as much as they had last night—but for an altogether different reason. Jared raked a hand through his hair. No matter how much he cared for Ava he wasn't going to allow her to weaken him as she'd already weakened his resolve. "I won't forgive him if that's what you're asking."

A melancholy frown flittered across her features. "What about me, then?"

Jared released a heavy sigh. "Ava—"

"Hi, Mama. Hi Jared."

Skipping out the door came his sweet-faced daughter. She looked from him to Ava, her brows lifted in wonder. Not wanting her to pick up on the tension between them he forced a smile and held out his hand to her. "Good morning, Little Star."

She went to him instantly as if she knew to whom she belonged. "I wanna go to the lake today."

"The lake, huh?"

"I wanna see my froggies."

Ava stood up and forced on a smile of her own. "I'll take you this afternoon, Lil."

"No," Jared said quickly, lifting Lily into his arms, holding her tightly. "*We'll* take you."

The little girl squealed with delight and buried her face in his chest.

"Rain's coming."

"How do you know, Mama?"

The three of them sat under a crabapple tree, the sky above unsure of its conclusion. Grayish clouds wandered across the pale sky and below a picnic basket sat open displaying several half-eaten turkey sandwiches and three empty bottles of lemonade.

Ava glanced over at Jared. "Jared taught me how to see rain in the clouds, Lil."

Lily's eyes widened and she whirled to face Jared. "How?"

"Look up," he said, pointing to a puffy cloud. "Can you see those gray steaks across that cloud?"

She nodded excitedly.

"That's rain."

"How'd you learn that?"

"It's something my grandmother taught me. And her ancestors taught her."

"I wish I had *antsisters,*" Lily said, flopping back on the red blanket.

"Sweetie, you do," Ava assured her, giving her exposed belly a tickle. "Rita and…Grandpa."

Lily grabbed Jared's hand. "How many antsisters you got, Jared?"

"Hundreds, I expect."

"I want hundreds, too."

"Well," he said, giving her a loving smile. "You can have mine, Little Star."

"Really?" she asked, bolting upright.

He looked pointedly at Ava. "Yes."

Looking pleased as punch, Lily scrambled to her feet and skipped off down the hill, following a butterfly to the water's edge.

For a few minutes neither Ava nor Jared spoke, just stared down at where Lily was searching for her frog.

Perhaps they, too, were searching—for words, for understanding of one another.

"We have to tell her," Jared said, breaking the silence, his gaze resolute. "She should know where she comes from."

"I know."

Ava hesitated, her chest tight with nerves. She was finally starting to realize why she'd come back here. To face the truth. Everyone's truth. It seemed that all involved in this past devastation were looking for answers.

Jared was right. It was time.

Her gaze moved over to him. He, too, deserved the full story. He deserved to know about the deal she'd made with her father and why she'd really left Paradise.

Her stomach dipped. He would never see her actions as an act of love, as her sacrifice for him.

"I won't wait much longer, Ava."

"I know," she said before turning back to watch their daughter play.

"Tomorrow I leave for a showing of my bags in San Antonio."

"That sounds like fun, Muna," Ava said, admiring the beautiful works of art Muna had set up on the dining room table after dinner that night.

"I feel good about this showing. I have many pieces I wish to see placed."

"These are amazing." Ava fingered a red and yellow jug-like basket. "I'm sure you'll sell the lot."

"It is not about the selling." Taking a seat at the table, Muna tossed her braids over her shoulders.

Jared grinned at Ava. "It's about the placement of her pieces. Making sure they find their way home."

Ava lifted a brow. "Home?"

"Each bag has an owner before it's finished."

"Really?"

With gentle reverence, Muna picked up a double woven basket in three shades of blue and held it to her heart. "When this basket was just reeds and plants it was in its rawest, truest state. Only then can it become truly attached to its rightful match."

Rawest, truest state, Ava mused. Muna could've been talking about her and Jared. "And how does its rightful match find the basket? How do they know each other?"

"They sense a need in each other. A need only the two can fill." Muna smiled first at Ava then at Jared, then rose gracefully from her chair. "Good night, my children," she said, before placing her basket back in its rightful spot on the table and leaving the room.

Rain fell from the sky in fine, misty sheets as Jared walked the path leading to his sweat lodge. It felt good to be outside, felt better to be taken over by the dance of rain than to remain inside another minute.

One hour ago he'd been standing between Muna and Ava, feeling the unspoken dialogue that had electrified the air around them all with the discussion of rightful matches. One by one they'd all dispersed, leaving the unidentified but uncomfortable energy behind in the dining room, no doubt hoping it wouldn't follow them.

Muna had gone to Lily's room, where the little girl had requested several stories before bed. Ava had retired to her room and Jared had gone to his office where for exactly two hours he'd pored over his work. Then a file had crossed his desk. A family of three: father, mother and daughter. They wanted to work on securing their financial future. They'd reminded him of his own odd family situation and he'd grown impatient and had headed out for a sweat.

But before he left the house, he'd stood outside Ava's door and fought the urge to knock.

Above him, the rain swelled to heavy droplets. His sweat lodge came into view and Jared broke out into a sprint toward the door.

He was so tired of fighting his attraction, his need for Ava. Why couldn't he just shout it to the world, admit that he craved her, plain and simple, admit that if she decided to move back to Paradise he wouldn't stop himself from seeing her, making love to her whenever she'd have him.

The tarp door to the lodge had been tossed up over the roof and Jared paused before entering. The last time he'd been here he'd walked away from Ava. Had she left the tarp this way? he wondered, stepping inside the dim cave.

His answer came quick and in the form of the sexiest, most knee-weakening sight he'd ever seen.

Ava.

There she was. Smiling at him, completely nude, her long blond hair loose about her shoulders and breasts. Standing above the cold rocks that were intermingled with several flickering candles.

The sight made his chest constrict.

Long ago, he'd talked about making love to her in a sweat lodge. Long ago, when they'd lain in each other's arms, her leg draped over his burgeoning arousal. Long ago, in that little shack on her father's land with the scent of hay and earth surrounding them.

Long ago…

It was useless to struggle, foolish to make conversation. Jared stripped off his clothes, went to her, stood before her. "I am in my rawest, truest form," he said with a hint of a smile.

She returned his smile, her green eyes dancing. "Me, too."

Jared reached out, brushed his fingertips over one perfect breast, then cupped the weighty underside and growled with desire. "You are so beautiful."

Her smile went soft and she said with the utmost sincerity, "Thank you."

"I'm glad you came back here."

"We have some unfinished business, I think."

"Yes." He touched her face, brushed a thumb over her lips. Lips he'd dreamed about, fantasized about for four long years. "This place is very special to me. It is where I pray, where I dance."

"And where you make love?" she said quickly, apprehension flickering in her eyes.

Jared leaned in and his mouth brushed her as he spoke. "I have never made love to a woman here."

Ava felt like melting against him, nuzzling her head into the curve of his shoulder, finding that familiar protection once again. But the velvet warmth of his mouth beckoned. She kissed him with a hunger she'd been suppressing for so long, raking her hands up his smooth, hard chest to his neck.

She couldn't believe her pluck in coming here, standing in the middle of Jared's sacred place completely nude and practically begging him to make love to her.

But those were the actions of a woman very much in love.

As were these, she mused, dragging her fingers up

the sides of his face and into his hair. The inky black-
ness felt like silk as it weaved through her fingers.

Jared pulled away for just a moment, gazed into her
eyes. As they stood there together, totally exposed, Ava
could almost hear the haunting streams of the Native
American flute. The sound thrummed in her chest, in
her womb.

"My spirit dances with yours," Jared said, raw hunger glittering in his eyes.

A hunger Ava understood.

With all the passion that filled her soul, she eased
his head back and kissed all the way down his neck.
His pulse pounded at the base of his throat and she
lapped at it with her tongue.

Jared cursed to the ceiling and she felt him hard
against her belly.

Reveling in her effect on him, Ava lowered her head
to his chest and took his nipple into her mouth and
between her teeth, tugging. Jared growled, squeezing
her breast in his palm as he pressed his hips against
her, hard, his rhythm furious.

Ava felt as though she were melting from the inside
out, completely liquid. It had always been primitive
with them, in sound and action, and she loved it.

Pressing him back slightly, she reached down and
encircled his shaft with her hand. On a groan, Jared
grabbed her wrist. Their eyes met in the dim light and
he gave her dangerous grin, using the force of his own
hand to lift hers, and himself, up and down—first
slowly, then faster. As she played his erection, his
breathing became rapid, his eyes glazed and he uttered
words and phrases that were meant to shock.

But they only aroused her more.

He pulsated in her hand, growing impossibly harder,

the wetness that leaked from him a tantalizing lubricant. His excitement made Ava squirm with need, her hips thrusting again and again as sweat dripped down her back.

Suddenly Jared released his grip on her hand and moved his palm down her belly. Down, down, until he was between her thighs. Slowly, decadently, he eased a finger between her wet curls, then slipped inside her.

Ava cried out and her fist tightened around him.

"I can't wait any longer," she whispered, her voice hoarse. "Don't make me wait any longer. Don't make me beg, Jared."

"Do you want this?" he said, drawing his finger out of her body, then thrusting it back in. "To be me?"

She sucked in a breath. "Yes."

He guided her back, laid her down on the smoky, sage-scented rug on the earth floor. "You will come with me?"

She nodded for she couldn't speak. Her body wouldn't allow it as it waited in anticipation for what it craved.

After sheathing himself, Jared positioned himself over her. He entered her slowly, his eyes locked on hers. There was something behind his gray gaze, she realized through a haze of desire. Something sad, but sweet at the same time and she felt like crying as she stared up at him.

The intensity between them ran so thick that Ava wanted to look away. But she knew she mustn't.

Love flowed through her veins as he began to move inside her. She wrapped her legs around his waist, pressed up to meet him. At first his strokes were languid, a dance she recalled so vividly, then they grew quicker.

Sweat beaded on Jared's forehead as he worked her body with his own.

"I remember this," he uttered, reaching underneath her buttocks and lifting her hips.

This time Ava let the tears come, let them escape the corners of her eyes and drip down her cheekbones. She remembered, too. As though time had never passed.

Lord, how could he ever know how much he was loved?

Rain pounded on the roof of the sweat lodge like tribal drums, and Jared matched its pace. Deep in her womb, Ava throbbed. Ached. She was in agony and holding on to her climax was nearly impossible.

She called out, called his name and gave in, shuddering, convulsing around him.

"Ava... *Na'hesta,*" he uttered with guttural intensity as he drove into her with one last deep thrust, before following her over the edge.

He collapsed on top of her, his breathing labored, his skin so warm and protective over hers she wished they could remain that way forever, all night or for as long as possible.

In the comfort of his arms, Ava couldn't help but wonder about what would happen next, what would be said—if Jared would get up and leave without a word. But her fears were quickly allayed when he rolled to the side, gathered her in his arms and held her tightly against him.

She released a weighty breath.

One she'd been holding in her lungs since the day she'd left Paradise.

Listening to the sound of his heart beating in his chest—first hectic, then slow, Ava let herself relax, let herself sleep, completely at peace.

Ten

"**I** want to take Lily."

Under a beautiful blue morning sky, Ava sat beside Jared and their daughter on the porch swing of the Redwolf Ranch house as her sister proposed the idea of baby-sitting Lily for a few nights.

"C'mon, sis," Rita said, crossing her arms of her chest.

"Are you bringing her to Dad's?" Ava asked, keeping her voice neutral for Lily's sake, but shooting her sister a look of caution.

"We all want to spend some time with her. And I can bring her to the wedding rehearsal myself."

"Rita, she was sick and—"

"She's not sick anymore—" she tossed her niece an exaggerated wink "—are you, pumpkin?"

Lily shook her head as she bounced up and down on Jared's knee. "Nope."

"See there," Rita said, leaning back against the wood railing. "I want to get to know her. So does Dad."

Ava flinched, she couldn't help it. Such a reaction had become instinctual. Of course, she wanted Lily to know her family, spend time with them, but there were things to take into consideration. One was her father. Without Ava around would he still be loving and gentle with her daughter? And two... With Lily and Muna away, there was no reason for her to stay at Redwolf Ranch.

Last night had been wonderful, except for the fact that they'd left the sweat lodge and headed home to separate rooms, separate beds. She would've loved a chance to wake up in his arms just once.

She looked pointedly at Rita. "You'll constantly supervise? I don't want any comments about the past—"

"No problem," Rita assured her. "Total supervision."

Her lips a little tight, Ava gave her daughter a smile. "Do you want to have a sleep over at Auntie Rita's and go see Grandpa?"

"Yes, yes, yes!" Lily exclaimed.

Her heart melted at the excitement in her daughter's face. Who knew? Ava thought. After this wedding, life could, and probably would, return to normal. Back to New York, away from her family. Lily wanted time with them. She deserved to have that time.

"All right," Ava said, tousling Lily's hair. "But just for two nights."

"Yea!" the little girl shouted. "Grandpa's house!"

"This okay with you, Jared?" Rita asked.

Jared looked at Ava, his gaze unreadable, then he

looked down at his smiling, animated daughter and said, "Of course."

Lily snuggled into Jared's chest. "You'll call me when Tayka has her baby?"

"Of course, Little Star." He kissed the top of her head. "You go and have fun with your grandpa and aunt Rita."

Jared kicked his feet up on the desk, ignoring his lawyer's comments, advice and objections as they spewed out one by one over the speakerphone. "You're not hearing me, Blake."

"But have you considered the overhead for a place like that?" the man asked.

"Of course I have." It was Jared's job to know such things. And granted, if a client of his came looking for advice on buying an old wreck of a ranch, he'd steer them in a different direction, too. But this wasn't about profit or good investment. "I want it, Blake. I don't care how much it is."

"Mr. Redwolf, please listen—"

With an audible curse, Jared dropped his feet from the steel desk and wrenched himself forward. "Just get me that ranch." Then stabbed the disconnect button.

"What are you doing?"

Jared glanced up. Looking lovely in a white blouse and tan pants, her blond curls piled on top of her head, Ava stood in the doorway, her brows drawn together in a worried frown.

"Just business," he said tightly.

"Buying another ranch?"

"Could be."

"Where?" She walked into the room and up to his desk.

Guilt pricked at him, but he shoved it aside. There was no way he was going to feel guilty about taking that man's property. Not after what he'd done. Not after the years of planning, of plotting a retribution that was sure to bring Jared some sense of relief. "The ranch is here in Paradise. Out on Raven Trail."

A deep frown creased her forehead. "On Raven Trail? But that's where our place—"

"Ava—"

"Why would you want that ranch?"

"You know why," he ground out, standing up, coming around his desk.

"Yes, I suppose I do." With shaky fingers, she brushed a phantom hair from her blouse. "But it's not even for sale yet. Dad hasn't decided—"

"I'm afraid he won't have much of a choice. The bank is ready to foreclose." The words felt like smooth, delicious honey in his mouth.

Her eyes searched his. "How do you know all this?"

"I have connections."

They stood so close, just as they had last night. Except this time, they were fully clothed and masked in their own bitterness and grief.

"Makes you happy to ruin him, doesn't it?" she said quietly.

"Yes." Jared didn't like the look in her eyes. She wasn't angry, she was confused and hurt and he was the cause. That fact filled him with little pride. But he pressed on as though some demon possessed his heart. "I refuse to allow his misdeeds to go unpunished."

"Well, good luck to you." She gave him a melancholy smile. "I just came to say goodbye and to thank you for the hospitality."

"What do you mean?"

"I'm all packed up and ready to go."

An invisible vise gripped his chest. "Where are you going?"

"Home."

"To New York?" He could barely spit out the words as anger rippled through him.

She shook her head. "No, to Rita's."

Mild relief sank its teeth into the anger and he leaned back against his desk. "Don't you want to spend some time over at your father's place, too?"

"You mean while it's still his?"

"Ava, the ranch is going to go to someone."

"I know, but are you the truest person for it? Are you meant for that place?"

He made a dismissive gesture with his hand. "You sound like Muna."

"She's a wise woman."

"She is overly forgiving."

Ava didn't respond, didn't move. Her gaze remained on his as if she was urging him to take it all back, to forgive and forget.

But he wasn't about to do that, either.

She nodded. "I'll see you at the wedding, Jared." Then she turned and walked to the door.

She was already in the hall when Jared caught up with her, took her hand. "Don't go."

"What?"

"Stay here with me." He didn't understand this desperate need he had for her. It just seemed that the closer he got to his revenge, the closer he wanted to cleave to Ava.

"Why?" She shook her head. "Lily's gone."

He lifted her hand to his mouth, kissed her palm. "Stay with me. Not for our daughter, but for me."

He'd never seen such a struggle go on behind two beautiful green eyes. But he understood it. He felt it, too.

"Like old times or something?" she asked on a dry chuckle.

"No—" he pulled her into his arms "—like new times. I've imagined so much in the past few years. Of you and I in this house alone."

On a weary sigh, she sagged against him, her voice aching with need. "I want to…"

"Then do." He held her against him, pressing her head to his shoulder. "For the next two days, let's erase the past four years. Let's eat, drink, make love and talk of long ago and of yesterday."

"Okay." She whispered the word into his neck, her soft lips pressing against his racing pulse.

It was close to midnight, the bewitching hour, when Jared slid deep inside her body. Her back to his charcoal sheets, Ava squeezed her buttocks tight and pressed her hips up to meet him. She didn't call out though, didn't make a sound. She wanted every last bit of pleasure that would complete their two day holiday to remain beneath her skin, where she could hold on to it forever.

Above her, Jared had his head thrown back, his chest rippled with hard, cut muscle and beaded with sweat. Ava let her gaze travel down his belly, down to where black hair ran in a thin line, down farther to where they were joined, wet and pink.

It was a beautiful sight.

She wanted to take their lovemaking slow, lose herself in the climax that was creeping up on her, winding through her body like a restless snake.

But Jared had other ideas.

He took his hand and ran it down her torso, slipped a finger between the V of hair at her core and stroked the hot, wet bundle of nerves he found there.

Heat shocked her senses, pleasure exploded throughout the tunnel of her body.

It was too much for any woman to bear.

Ava released the moan that had been waiting in her lungs. She arched her back, feeling her nipples tighten and ache as the hot current of orgasm sparked through her womb, down her legs and back up again. She felt her feminine muscle fist around Jared, pulsate around him, urging him to join her until at last he did.

Ava wrapped her arms around his neck as he dropped on top of her, his breathing ragged.

She stared up at the ceiling of his bedroom with its tribal, textured paintings and heavily woven, brightly colored tapestries. It was so him. Raw, dangerous, vivid.

Beside the bed the phone rang, jarring Ava from her thoughts. Jared ignored it, kissing her neck with lingering passion. But Ava felt compelled to say, "It could be about Lily."

With a rush of breath, Jared was up and off of her in one second. "Of course. I need to get used to that." He gave her a wide grin, then picked up the phone, glancing at the caller ID. "No, it's just my lawyer. Business has no hours."

In one instant, the romance and the intimacy of the moment were lost. Ava felt like sinking into the mattress. "Right."

Jared rested above her, his weight on his arms, his eyes imploring her. "Ava, let's not—"

"You shouldn't do this," she said quickly, without thinking.

"Shouldn't do what?"

"Don't buy our ranch, Jared."

The tenderness in his expression died right there. He sat back, ground out, "So it's 'our' ranch now, is it?"

Ava sat up, too, holding the gray sheet to her breasts. "This isn't about my dad. This isn't about saving him."

"Sounds that way."

"It's about you."

"I don't need to be saved."

She reached out, touched his face. "Can't we let the past go? Both of us. Let it go? Isn't it better to rejoice in what we have now?"

"And what is that?" he asked, eyebrow arched.

Ava paused, biting her lip. She didn't know what they had, she only knew what she felt and if she didn't say it now she'd never respect herself. "I love you, Jared. I've never stopped loving you." She sat up taller, lifting her chin. "I've made some mistakes. Some whoppers. But I'm hoping you can forgive me."

His mouth was set in a grim line. "And your father? Must I forgive him, too?"

"Don't you think your anger might be slightly misplaced?"

"No."

"Yes, he kicked you off the land. Yes, he was a bigot and—"

"Was?"

"Yes, was." She swallowed hard and hoped she was doing the right thing, knowing she had no choice—her conscience demanded her to be completely truthful.

"But I didn't leave because he made me. Not completely."

Moonlight bathed the room in pale white, illuminating Jared's ruthless expression and hard mouth.

"When my father found out I was pregnant," she said, her heart slamming against her ribs. "He ordered me to go to New York. But I refused."

His gaze glittered cold and impatient.

"I refused until…"

"Until what?"

"Until he told me that he would kick you and Muna out onto the street if I didn't leave." She inhaled deeply and knew that what she was about to say next might truly be the end of them. "Maybe I didn't believe in you. Maybe I didn't think you could take care of all of us. I don't know. I'm not sure. I was really scared back then. But I do know one thing, the main reason I left was to protect those that I loved. Muna, Lily and you."

There, she'd said it. Everything was out in the open. She held no more lies in her heart.

She watched the realization of her words come over him.

"You're right, Ava," he said finally, his features hard and unyielding. "My anger has been misplaced. All this time I thought you'd left because he'd forced you."

"I wanted to come to you and tell you—"

"That you didn't think I could support you and our child?"

She inched toward him on the bed. "Jared, you were just starting out, working your way up. I didn't want to get in the way of that. I didn't want to burden you—"

"Our child was a burden?"

"No! Please try to understand my state of mind. I loved you so much. I wanted you and Muna to be okay."

"You're packed and ready to go?"

Ava froze at his words, shriveled a little at his expression. The love of her life was looking at her with pure hatred and she wanted to fling herself into his arms and shake him until he understood. She choked back the sob that maliciously tickled her throat and muttered, "Yes."

"Then maybe you should go."

She nodded slowly, then swung her legs over the side of the bed and stood up, taking the sheet with her. "All right, Jared. I'll go. But know this. For whatever it's worth, I love you so much and I am deeply sorry for everything that's happened. You'll never know how sorry. But there's nothing anyone can do to change the past. Not me, not my father or his ranch—"

"Holy sh—" Jared came to an abrupt halt, regarded her with a critical squint. "Did you sleep with me to save your father's ranch?"

Tears pricked Ava's eyes and she felt sick to her stomach. She had to get out of his room, his house, his life. "I'm going home now," she said, gathering up her clothes with shaky hands. "Lily will always be yours and always be in your life. I, however, will not."

On legs weakened by harsh words, she left the room.

Eleven

———

Dawn broke earlier than usual but Jared was too hung-over to notice.

After Ava wlked out last night, he'd walked up—up to his office and straight to the bar. Of course, drowning himself in whiskey hadn't been the smartest thing he'd done all year, but it sure had blotted out the past few days. For six or seven precious hours he'd lain against the cool surface of his desk and drifted off into sweet oblivion, forgetting about Ava, about making love to her and about sending her away with his unforgiving boorishness and one very harsh question.

He raked his hands through his hair, then leaned back in his chair. Where had that question come from? Hell, he knew she hadn't slept with him to save Ben's ranch. She was in love with him. Still, after all these years. He'd seen that love in her eyes from the moment they'd bumped into each other at Benton's Bridal. In fact, he'd found great pleasure in the fact.

He'd accused her because he'd wanted to hurt her. And he had.

Pride didn't fill his empty gut, only a deep sense of regret. But regret wasn't wise now, he reminded himself. He needed to find his way back to resentment—and vigilance. After last night, Ava might just be mad enough to take Lily back to New York without talking to him first.

He couldn't allow that.

"You are acting like a child, Jared Redwolf."

Jared groaned, glancing at the old woman walking through his office door. She had returned home before sun-up, taken meditation to the hills, then had obviously spoken to Ava or Rita while she drank her herbal tea.

"Muna, please," he said, his voice tired. "You don't understand."

She stood in front of his desk, seeming far taller than her mere five feet four inches. "Your pride has been hurt, this I understand."

"She lied to me over and over."

"She was wrong and afraid to hurt you further. Has she not admitted this?"

"She has, but—"

"You do not forgive her? The mother of your child?"

"Muna—" he began, his tone laced with warning.

"You will not forgive him, either?" she continued, her eyes dark with frustration and disappointment. "The grandfather of your child?"

"Dammit, Muna—"

"I will not be silent while you ruin your life once again."

"It was they who ruined my life."

"Take responsibility for your part in this, Jared. Come to terms with your interminable anger over your father's misdeeds, or you will be a very lonely man."

With gritted teeth, Jared turned away and stared out at his property, the world he'd created for himself and for Ava, if he ever had the guts to admit it.

As if reading his mind, Muna said gently, "You still love her. More than ever, I think."

"I have work to do," he grumbled.

"Yes, you do. More than you will ever know."

Muna said no more, gave her grandson no further expressions of irritation as she walked out of the room.

What the hell did she want from him? To forget the past? Forget everyone involved? All that was done to him? Taken from him?

Did she want him to go find Ava and tell her he loved her still—more than ever?

"Not a chance," he said, his tongue heavy with contempt.

He pushed out of his chair to his feet and headed for the door. His office smelled stale suddenly. He needed air, clean air.

He took the stairs two at a time, punched open the screen door and stepped out onto the porch. But no sweet morning air met his lungs, for he didn't take the time to inhale. He was far too distracted. Speeding up the driveway, dust clouds at his rear, was Ben Thompson.

Jared cursed as the Ford Bronco came to a screeching halt in front of the house, sending gravel flying every which way. He hadn't seen the man in a while.

After Ben's accident, Jared had just ignored him whenever their paths crossed in town.

Ben had barely shut the car door before he started up the stairs and in on Jared. "You can take my land, Redwolf. For everything that I've done to you and yours, I don't blame you. But hurting Ava—"

"Hold it right there," Jared interrupted, stopping the man from progressing farther than the porch steps. "Whatever goes on between me and Ava and is none of your business."

"She's my daughter."

"Since when?"

Ben stiffened, the lines around his eyes deepening with a frown. "You'll learn that being a father is both rewarding and complicated, especially when you push your own foolish, pigheaded ideas on the ones you love."

Jared snorted with derision. "I don't think I'll be taking parenting tips from you."

"Fine, fine." Ben ripped off his Stetson and swatted the brim against his jeans. Dust floated in the air around him. "But you're making an even bigger mistake than I did, Jared."

"It's Mr. Redwolf," he said with scalding hostility.

Shaking his head, Ben said, "Revenge is a lonely business."

Jared's nostrils flared with annoyance. First Muna, now Ben Thompson. "I've been alone a long time. I'm used to it."

"Maybe, but is that the legacy you want to leave Lily?"

Jared stepped forward and got in the old man's face. "Don't talk about my child. Don't you ever talk about my child. You have no right after what you've pulled."

A flash of desolation darkened Ben's gaze. "True. Too true."

"Damn right it is." He eyeballed Ben, enjoying the moment and the words he'd always longed to say, "Now get the hell off my land."

Ben Thompson gave him a sad, understanding nod, then turned around and walked to his truck. "Just one more thing, Mr. Redwolf," he said, climbing into the truck's cab.

"What's that?"

"I'm real sorry for who I used to be. And for kicking you and Muna out. But my biggest regrets will always be taking away my daughter's options when I found out she was pregnant and for taking away your chance to see your baby born." He climbed into the truck, slammed the door and said out the window, "Every man deserves that."

As he watched Ben Thompson tool down the dusty driveway, Jared clung desperately to the hatred in his heart. But deep inside, the steady rhythmic drums of another unspeakable emotion threatened to devour that pitiable hatred whole.

It was five o'clock, Ava noted.

The wedding rehearsal was supposed to have begun an hour ago.

As the sun pondered the idea of dipping into the horizon, Ava sat amongst family and close friends at the lovely lakeside spot that Rita had chosen for her ceremony. A spread of bread, cheese and honey ham waited to be devoured beside the fifty or so chairs under a shady tree. And seated in the front row, Ava smoothed her blue silk dress and wished that the women in back of her would just shut up.

But no such luck.

"Where's the groom?" Tilly Edwards whispered.

Gladys Mason, the wedding singer and the only woman in Paradise with a platinum-blond beehive, giggled like a schoolgirl. "Maybe he's a no-show."

"Oh, Gladys that's terrible."

"But true it seems."

"Poor, poor Rita," Tilly said with a cluck of her tongue. "Her family has known such sorrow."

At that, Ava stood up and scooched to the end of the aisle. Busybodies! she grumbled to herself as she faced both women and tossed them the stink eye. Tilly and Gladys stained pink and dropped their gazes, clearly ready to be thoroughly dressed down. But Ava didn't bother, just walked past them without further incident. After all, she mused, the two weren't worth her reprimand. She needed to find her sister.

She spotted Rita down by the water's edge, sitting under a tree calmly sipping a diet soda, and headed that way.

"Hey," she said, plopping down beside her.

Rita gave her a smile. "Hey, yourself."

"You look calm."

She shrugged. "I feel calm."

"People are talking, little sister."

"About Sakir not being here, you mean?"

"Uh, yeah." Ava chuckled lightly.

"Well, let them. I couldn't care less what old beehive and her crew have to say." She drained her soda and sighed. "Sakir just called and he's stuck in Boston on business. He'll be here tomorrow."

"What about his family?"

"They're stuck in Emand."

"Business as well?" Ava asked, her brows drifting upward.

"Yep."

Ava felt a hitch in her belly. Rita's explanation sounded incredibly fishy, as did her attitude. Most brides would be freaking out if their groom wasn't at the rehearsal. But Rita had never really been the freaking out sort...

"Okay, little sister," Ava said finally.

"You say that like you don't believe me."

"Rita, I just want you to have the perfect day, that's all."

"Don't worry," she said, patting Ava's hand. "He just called me and apologized—" she smiled brightly "—and told me he loved me. He's really busy, you know. He said to go ahead with the rehearsal and I can fill him in tomorrow."

Ava so desperately wanted to ask her sister questions about this man, let her know that she felt this was a shady deal and that perhaps Sakir wasn't the right man for her—business or not. But she bit her tongue. She'd seen too many families break up over opinions regarding a loved one, including her own regarding Jared, and she wasn't about to alienate her sister.

She would just be there for Rita no matter what happened tomorrow. "All right, but we need to get this thing started."

Rita stood up and offered her sister a hand. "Let's go through the ceremony then."

Pulled to her feet, Ava asked, "Who'll play the groom's part? Beehive? Tilly?"

A sly smile erupted on Rita's face. "Maybe Jared could."

"Not funny."

"I wasn't being funny." She glanced passed Ava, raising a brow. "Would you mind, Jared?"

"No problem."

Ava's breath caught in her throat and she whirled around. There he was, framed by the flowered archway in the distance, looking ruggedly handsome in a pair of blue jeans and a crisp black shirt, his hair pulled back in a ponytail.

"Making sure I haven't skipped town?" she asked a little tightly.

His gray eyes darkened. "I must protect what's mine, Ava. You know that."

"I do know, but I promised you Lily would always be in your life." A thick ache took up residence in Ava's throat and she wanted to kick herself for getting so emotional. Especially after she'd spent all night trying to rid Jared from her thoughts, heart and mind. "After all," she continued, "I've already called my office and quit my job so we can move out here permanently, so Lily can be near her father."

Jared's jaw dropped a fraction. "Did you?"

"Yes, I did."

He shook his head, his eyes softening. "Ava..."

"So no need to check up on me, okay?" she said, starting past him.

He grabbed her wrist, turned her back with gentle resolve. "I didn't come here to check up on you. Thought about it." He gave her a grim smile. "But I didn't. Actually Muna and I came to watch the rehearsal—" he nodded at Rita "—on insistence from your sister."

Ava turned on Rita, glared at her. "Excuse me?"

"Listen, guys," Rita began, laughing nervously, pointing at the guests and waiting preacher. "Everyone's waiting. Why don't you two play Sakir and I up at the altar.''

"What?" Jared fairly choked.

"Rita Willow Thompson—" Ava began in warning.

Rita shrugged. "It would be a little weird being up there with a man other than Sakir.''

A stuttered chuckle erupted in Ava's throat. "You've got to be kidding.''

"C'mon, sis," Rita begged, batting her pale lashes in her sister's direction. "Pretty please. Please Jared. Save me from further embarrassment? It can be my wedding gift.''

Both Ava and Jared stared at Rita like she was nuts for such a suggestion. Or a royal pain in the match-making butt. Ava was ready to tell her sister to go jump in the lake, that the last thing Jared wanted to give as a gift was standing up in front of preacher with her, but Jared's tug on her arm stopped her.

"Let's just get it over with," he muttered, tugging Ava toward the crowd.

With a strange little squeal, Rita took off toward the crowd, calling out for them to take their places and explaining her situation. Jared and Ava made their way over to the front of the aisle and waited for the music to begin. They said nothing, stood close, but didn't touch. Finally Lily picked up her basket and started down the aisle, sprinkling leaves as her flowers. Ava felt Jared move closer to her and when she looked up at him, he smiled, a shared tenderness in his eyes.

It's for our daughter, she reminded herself as they walked down the aisle toward the preacher. He loves Lily, not her mother and the sooner she got that through her swollen heart the better.

"Dearly beloved," the preacher began, his voice

booming through the wild lushness of the landscape. "We are gathered together today to celebrate the love between this man and this woman."

Ava felt weak suddenly. The man's words invaded her soul. How many times had she dreamt of such a moment? Marrying Jared, telling him that she loved him more than anything—all in front of this dusty old town and the man who had kept them apart for so long.

"Love is such a gift, such a blessing. Love is patient and kind. Love heals and rebuilds." The preacher smiled at Ava, then at Jared. "These two souls clearly belong together, anyone can see that."

It was impossible not to look at Jared, standing before her, his intense stare causing her stomach to ache with longing.

"When we take marriage vows," the preacher continued. "We enter into a union of such depth, such vulnerability it can be a bit frightening. But no great rewards can ever come without one great leap of faith."

The words spoke such volumes to her, and Ava wondered if Jared could hear them, too, through his anger and pain.

"Do you take this woman to be your wife?" the preacher asked.

A clear struggle was being played out behind Jared's eyes. Every emotion she'd heard named passed through. But finally, he uttered a firm, "I do."

"And do you take this man to be your husband?"

Ava felt no struggle and she wanted him to see that. She nodded, her throat tight with all the love she'd held silent in her heart. "Yes, I do. So much."

Muffled laughter rose up from the small congregation. But between Ava and Jared there was only a profound silence.

"The rings will be exchanged here and the verses that accompany them." The man searched his book, then grinned. "Ah, yes. Is there anyone here who can see just cause for these two not to be joined?"

Jared didn't speak, didn't take his eyes off her. Ava, too, had her gaze locked. She tried to pretend that this was real, just for now. And that tonight, they would share a bed as husband and wife.

"By the power vested in me, I pronounce you husband and wife." The preacher grinned at Jared, leaned in and whispered, "You may kiss your lovely bride."

Ava stood stock-still. She wanted so badly for him to kiss her. For him to forgive her and his past, and want her again, want this. Marriage, a lifelong friendship, their child and the others to come—the others with his eyes and her capacity for love.

A sad smile itched at Jared's beautiful mouth. "We'll wait until our wedding day."

Ava felt tears in her throat, but forced them back. She was not going to cry. She'd given in to tears way too many times since she'd been back. She lifted her chin, gave Jared her hand and let him lead her down the aisle.

Rita grinned as they approached. "The perfect bride and the perfect groom."

"I'm going to get something to drink," Ava said softly, dropping Jared's hand and leaving the two of them for the solace of the punch table.

But it wasn't solace for long.

"No more running away, *Nahtona*."

Muna was at her side, her hand on Ava's shoulder.

Now more than ever, Ava wished she could sag into the aging grandmother's arms and find some comfort.

"I'm not running anywhere this time," Ava said proudly. "Just giving your grandson the freedom he wants."

"That is not what he wants."

"Well, he sure doesn't want me."

"You're wrong."

A sudden gust of wind shot across the lake's surface, striking Ava's face. "Please excuse me, Muna. I need to see about Lily."

"When my grandson comes to you, listen to his heart with yours."

"Why do you think he'll come to me?"

"I know these things, *Nahtona.*"

Ava started to walk away, then paused. "Are you going to tell me what that word means?"

Muna smiled, then stood up on her tiptoes and kissed Ava's cheek. "It means 'my daughter.'"

Twelve

Jared got the call about Tayka just minutes after the rehearsal ended and had rushed home to find her in labor. Muna and Lily had followed in Ava's car, and were sitting beside him on the floor just outside of the stall as two vets helped the foal slip from her mother's body and into the world.

Lily jumped up from Jared's lap and squealed with delight at the amazing new life. "She's so pretty."

"She is at that," Jared agreed, glad he'd decided not to help in the foaling and had held his excited daughter in his arms as they watched. "I think we should call her Nala, what do you think?"

"I love it," Lily exclaimed, then turned to Ava. "Did I look like Nala when I was born, Mommy?"

Jared felt Ava's eyes on him as she spoke. "No, sweetie. You were pink and small and you smiled the moment I looked at you."

A deep ache gripped Jared's chest. He wanted so much to have been there, see his baby born, but that was over and done now. Lily was with him and he was lucky to have her.

As he watched the foal try to stand on her wobbly legs, he realized that his anger had dropped away. Sometime between the wedding rehearsal and the birth of Tayka's baby, the rage inside his heart had disappeared. And in its place had come a niggling sense of fear. Fear that these three people who surrounded him right now might cease to love him if he didn't get his act together.

His grandmother, his daughter and the woman he would love for eternity.

The preacher's words were forever imprinted on his soul. Love is a gift, one Jared realized he'd been throwing back in Ava's face from the first day he'd seen her. Love is patient, as he had refused to be. Love was kind, it made men forgive instead of crushing another's spirit under their boot heel.

And love was healing, a road that he was desperate to take.

"Who's that horse?" Lily asked, tugging Jared from his thoughts, pointing to a black stallion in the next stall.

Jared smiled down at her. "That's little Nala's papa."

"Oh."

"What's wrong, Little Star?" Muna asked as Lily frowned slightly.

"I wish I had a papa."

Jared looked over at Ava. Tears in her eyes, she smiled and nodded. It was time, time for their little girl to hear the truth.

"Sweetie," Ava began, giving her daughter a bright smile, "you do have a papa."

Lily's eyes widened. "I do?"

"Yes." Jared lifted her up and placed her back down in front of him, so she was looking directly into his eyes. "He's right in front of you, Lil."

The room got quiet, even Tayka and her foal seemed to still waiting for father and daughter to see each other. For an understanding to come.

As she stared up at him, Lily frowned, thoughtful. Then, like a beam of beautiful sunlight, comprehension dawned and she smiled, threw her arms around his neck and hummed.

"Are you glad, Little Star?" he asked, swallowing hard, biting back the first tears he'd allowed himself in twenty years.

Lily snuggled into his neck and whispered, "Every night, I wished upon a star that you might be my daddy, Jared."

"Your wish came true, then." He kissed her cheek. "And so did mine."

With Lily against him, Jared looked up into Ava's eyes, said, "There is much to be said. Much for me to explain and apologize for. Let's go up to the house and put our child to bed. Then we'll talk."

Her eyes bright with unshed tears, Ava nodded.

And beside her, Muna smiled.

After putting Lily to bed, Ava and Jared went outside and sat on the porch swing. As they rocked slowly back and forth, Ava breathed in the sweet night air and prayed for a happy ending to their conversation.

But regardless, she thought, this time she wasn't running away.

"I built this house for you, you know."

"What?" Ava turned to look at him, so breathtakingly handsome in the sliver of moonlight.

"Well, with you in mind," he amended, staring out at the abundance of land before him.

"The colors and the flowers are certainly me."

He shook his head. "Not just that." He turned to look at her, his eyes gentle. "I thought I was trying to forget you. But I realized that I was actually building you into my memory forever."

She smiled, took his hand. "I didn't need anything to do that."

"I love you, Ava," he said simply.

Her heart in her throat, she reached out and touched his face. "I love you, too."

"I always have and I always will."

Tears filled her eyes as she caressed his cheek with her fingertips.

He leaned into her palm, turned his head and kissed her hand. "I'm sorry."

"God, what do you have to be sorry for?"

"I didn't have a father, but I had a mother who I loved with all my heart. At eighteen, I would've done anything she asked of me whether I believed it was right or not." He drew her to him, held her face in his hands. "I'm sorry that I treated you with such an unforgiving spirit. It's not the Cheyenne way. And I don't want it to be mine. You are an amazing woman who only wanted the best for her child." He leaned in and kissed her softly. "Thank you for taking such good care of her. She is you, you know?"

"She is you, too." Tears streamed down Ava's cheeks, no doubt taking the mascara from her wet lashes with them. But she couldn't care less. Jared was

letting down his guard, letting his heart finally fly free.
"You forgive me?" she asked.

He nodded. "And do you forgive me?"

Through her tears, she managed a smile. "Of
course."

His gaze dropped for a moment, his voice softened.
"I'm not going to take your father's ranch."

"What?"

"I realized that it wasn't Ben I was angry with. Not
really. It was my father. It was my fear of becoming
him that made me lash out at everyone close to me,
turn those I loved most away." Jared sat back against
the wood swing. "I'm willing to talk to Ben, see who
he's become, maybe help him regain the land instead."

Ava just stared. "I thought—"

"You thought I wanted revenge?"

"Yes."

He shook his head. "Not anymore. Not for you and
for our daughter and our family. He's part of that family."

Her heart seemed to stand still. "What *do* you want
now then?"

"You."

She grinned, laughed with joy, threw herself into his
arms. "You've got me."

"You and Lily and the others we shall have."

"Yes."

"And next time," he said, his voice rough with emotion as he eased her back, looking deeply into her eyes.
"I'll be there helping you bring those children into the
world."

Tears rolled down her cheeks.

"Marry me, Ava?" he whispered against her lips.

"In a heartbeat," she whispered back.

He cupped the back of her neck, bringing her mouth to his, closer until he was a delicious blur.

His kiss was tender and open and completely loving.

Just as he, Ava mused with deep gratitude, had finally allowed himself to be.

*   *   *   *   *

Ava's sister Rita is about to walk down the aisle with her handsome boss...or is she? When Rita's scheming lands her with an unexpected groom on her wedding day, she gets a whole lot more than she bargained for— and finds her heart's desire!

Don't miss Laura Wright's next sizzling story,

A BED OF SAND

Coming in September 2004 only from Silhouette Books.

For a sneak peek, just turn the page!

Prologue

There is a place in the northern desert of Joona where a man can race his stallion straight into the coming sunset. A place where amber veins run through pale sand like a thousand snakes beneath your feet, and white rocks rise straight up into a seamless blue sky. A place where the air is scented with heat and spicy wild brush, and the gods—the watchers of this land—stand erect in their sacred pools and welcome all those who risk so much in coming here.

This place is Emand.

An ancient land, rich with oil, beautiful valleys and vast cultures. But a land great with sorrow and bitter hearts.

This land bore three sons before claiming their father. Though broken in spirit, the eldest son understood his position and remained in his homeland to rule. The younger son, destined to follow his great father, surrendered to the gods at just fifteen years of age. And the second son, Sheikh Sakir Ibn Yousef Al-Nayhal, left his home in search of his soul. But what he found instead was the strange deserts of Texas and the emptiness of a man who belonged nowhere and to no one.

One

"What a waste," Rita Thompson muttered, taking one last look at herself in the full-length mirror.

It was all there. Everything to be admired in a late-summer bride. Killer white dress—strapless, of course—white satin sandals to give her a little height, tuille veil to cover her anxious expression and a classy French manicure on both fingers and toes.

Fabulous.

And she hadn't forgotten those simple traditions of a bride-to-be, either. She'd assigned her eyes as the sacred "something blue" and her sister's pearl earrings as the "something borrowed." But when it came to the "something new," she'd decided to pass.

Hey, she'd foot the bill for this entire ceremony and the I'm-really-sorry-about-deceiving-all-of-you reception afterward. She wasn't about to pay for anything else. Especially for herself.

She grimaced at her wedding-white reflection. "Maybe someday, kid. If you're lucky."

"If who's lucky?"

Rita turned and saw her dad in the doorway of the Paradise Lake Lodge, looking very dapper in his dove-gray suit and matching boots. "Me. I'm lucky. Got a great family and I'm not too shy to say it."

"Rita, darlin'," he said, going to her, "you've never been too shy for anything."

A deep pang of guilt invaded Rita's heart as her father stood before her, his eyes so kind and loving. She'd never lied to him before. Sure, she'd omitted certain things as a rowdy teenager, but this situation was an entirely different matter. She'd directly deceived him. Hopefully he'd understand why she'd gone to all the trouble of faking her engagement and marriage, and forgive her.

"You look very handsome, Dad."

"Thank you. Thank you." He grinned and poked out his elbow in her direction. "Ready to be escorted down the aisle, beautiful lady?"

She returned his smile and slipped her arm through his. "As I'll ever be."

Ben Thompson squeezed her to him, seriousness creeping into his tone. "You're sure about this, right?"

"Of course."

He shrugged, said, "All righty," then led her down the lodge steps and out into the glorious sunshine and easy lake breeze.

"You know, I tried to have a little talk with your intended," he said. "But he hadn't arrived as yet. Cutting it pretty close, isn't he?"

"He's a very busy man."

"Maybe so, but I don't like it." He led her toward

the lakeside, where fifty or so guests sat in white chairs facing a lacy canopy. ''Not the best way to start off with a new family.''

''Don't worry. He's wonderful, Dad—and he'll be here.'' Interesting, she mused. She sounded completely convincing. Just the way a woman ready to take the plunge with the man of her dreams would sound.

Well, the *dreams* part was actually pretty accurate. She'd had a serious crush on her boss, Sheikh Sakir Al-Nayhal, for close to three years now. He was intelligent, intense and over-the-top sexy. Her type in a nutshell. But alas, the man didn't even know she was alive—below the neck, at any rate.

She was the best at what she did, an assistant to die for, and Sakir treated her as such, with the utmost respect. But he never looked at her as anything more than a highly competent business associate. At least, he'd never shown any signs of interest. No lengthy glances at her legs or knowing smiles when she'd worn something just a little bit revealing to work, hoping he'd notice.

Of course, that lack of interest was exactly why she'd chosen him as her mock-fiancé. Well, that and the fact that he rarely came to Paradise and was just this minute having a business lunch with Harvey Arnold in Boston—a lunch she'd set up two months ago.

''I still can't believe we haven't met him.'' Her father sighed as they reached the little staging area several yards from the altar. ''It's not right.''

''Save your breath, Dad.'' Ava, Rita's older sister, sidled up to them, looking like a goddess in her pale pink satin bridesmaid dress. ''Rita knows what she's doing.''

"Listen to my matron of honor, Dad."

"*Maid* of honor," Ava corrected with a smile. "For three more weeks, anyway."

Rita glanced past her sister to a gorgeous Cheyenne man sitting near the altar, his newly found daughter on his lap, and felt a deep sense of peace. She'd done it. This little bit of deceit had been worth everything. Ava was back with the man she loved, their daughter finally had a father and their marriage was just weeks away.

Rita gave her father's arm a squeeze. "Let's get this party started."

"Just waiting on the groom, daughter."

Rita mentally rolled her eyes. "He'll be coming out with the preacher."

Or not.

Her father led her to within feet of the white carpet stretched out over the grass, the carpet that led straight to the altar. Several of the guests turned, saw her, then dropped into a low hush. Beside her, the string quartet sat at attention, ready to play.

Rita took a deep breath, released it and clenched her fists around her sweaty palms. All she wanted to do was get this over with, get jilted and get going, off to New Orleans for beignets and hurricanes.

"There's Reverend Chapman," Ava whispered from beside her.

"Where?" their father asked.

"Right there, Dad. He's—" Ava stopped short.

"Holy hell," Ben said, his eyes narrowed. "He's alone. What the devil—"

"Dad, please." Ava touched her sister's shoulder and squeezed.

Rita lifted her chin. She was ready to hear the cheerless whispers of her friends and family as they realized her fiancé wasn't coming. She was ready to blush and force a few tears. She was ready to flee in shame.

Then suddenly her gaze caught on a decidedly male figure, proud as a prince and dressed in a white caftan, striding across the grass toward the lonely Reverend Chapman.

Rita's heart jolted, and she felt as weak as one of the reeds blowing against the lake's surface beyond.

This wasn't possible. Not possible.

But then again, there he was.

Her boss, her fictional fiancé and her bone-melting crush, Sakir Al-Nayhal, had arrived.

Uninvited and totally unabashed.

She watched him walk, stared as he came to stand at the altar, tall, broad and desperately gorgeous, his dark skin eating up the paleness of his caftan. Then he turned and looked down the aisle, straight at Rita, his black eyes and firm, sensual mouth humorless.

Rita swallowed hard as her mind raced and the world spun.

Sakir arched an eyebrow and thrust out a hand toward her as if commanding her to come to him.

"Wow," Ava said beside her. "I hadn't expected him to be so…"

Panic welling in her throat, Rita cursed under her breath and muttered, "And I hadn't expected him—period."

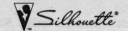

presents

You're on his hit list.

Enjoy the next title in

Katherine Garbera's
King of Hearts miniseries:

MISTRESS MINDED
(Silhouette Desire #1587)

When a workaholic boss persuades his faithful
assistant to pretend to be his temporary
mistress, it's going to take the influence of
a matchmaking angel-in-training to bring
them together permanently!

*Available June 2004
at your favorite retail outlet.*

Award-winning author

Jennifer Greene

**invites readers to indulge in
the next compelling installment of**

The Scent of Lavender

The Campbell sisters awaken to passion
when love blooms where they least expect it!

WILD IN THE MOONLIGHT

(Silhouette Desire #1588)

When sexy Cameron Lachlan walked onto
Violet Campbell's lavender farm, he seduced
the cautious beauty in the blink of an eye.
Their passion burned hot and fast, but
could they form a relationship beyond
the bedroom door?

*Available June 2004
at your favorite retail outlet.*

From *USA TODAY* bestselling author

Cait London

HOLD ME TIGHT

(Silhouette Desire #1589)

Jessica Sterling is concerned about a threat
to her best friend and is determined to secure
the best man for the job—unnervingly attractive
Alexi Stepanov. But Alexi is in no mood to take
orders from this sweet-talking siren, and decides
to make a few demands of his own....

HEART BREAKERS

*Available June 2004
at your favorite retail outlet.*

COMING NEXT MONTH

#1585 CHALLENGED BY THE SHEIKH—Kristi Gold
Dynasties: The Danforths
Hotshot workaholic Imogene Danforth was up for a promotion, and only
her inability to ride a horse was standing in her way. Sheikh Raf Shakir
had vowed to train her on one of his prized Arabians…provided she stay
at his ranch. But what was Raf truly training Imogene to be: a wonderful
rider or his new bed partner?

#1586 THE BRIDE TAMER—Ann Major
Forced to rely on her wealthy in-laws, Vivian Escobar never dreamed
she'd meet a man as devastatingly sexy as Cash McRay—a man who was
set to marry her sister-in-law but who only had eyes for Vivian. Dare they
act on the passion between them? For their secret affair might very well
destroy a family.…

#1587 MISTRESS MINDED—Katherine Garbera
King of Hearts
With a lucrative contract on the line, powerful executive Adam Powell
offered his sweet assistant the deal of a lifetime—pretend to be his
mistress until the deal was sealed. Jayne Montrose was no fool; she knew
this was the perfect opportunity to finally get into Adam's bed…and into
his heart!

#1588 WILD IN THE MOONLIGHT—Jennifer Greene
The Scent of Lavender
She had a gift for making things grow…except when it came to
relationships. Then Cameron Lachlan walked onto Violet Campbell's
lavender farm and seduced her in the blink of an eye. Their passion
burned hot and fast, but could their blossoming romance overcome the
secret Violet kept?

#1589 HOLD ME TIGHT—Cait London
Heartbreakers
Desperate to hire the protective skills of Alexi Stepanov, Jessica Sterling
found herself offering him anything he wanted. She never imagined his
price would be so high, or that she would be so willing to give him
everything he demanded…and more.

#1590 HOT CONTACT—Susan Crosby
Behind Closed Doors
On forced leave from the job that was essentially his entire life, Detective
Joe Vicente was intrigued by P.I. Arianna Alvarado's request for his help.
He agreed to aid in her investigation, vowing not to become personally
involved. But Joe soon realized that Arianna was a temptation he might
not be able to resist.

SDCNM0504